Coast

Black Hawk MC
Book Six

by Carson Mackenzie

Published by CM Books, LLC
Copyright © December 2019 Carson Mackenzie
Cover Design by Carson Mackenzie
ISBN# 978-1-952184-36-9
ISBN# 978-1-078761-16-1
ISBN# 978-1-656091-10-9

Synopsis

As one of the enforcers of the club, Emery "Coast" Cortez is used to others doing as he says, not out of fear, but with respect for him and the position he holds. His mixed-race has never been an issue with the club, but growing up, the outside world wasn't always as easily accepting of his Mexican/Native American ethnicity.

Coast learned at an early age to ignore the slurs, the derogatory statements and the presumptions made from his looks alone. Instead, focusing on the goals he set and single-mindedly reaching each one while others wasted their time trying to deter him. With his mind set on Mackenzie Minton, she doesn't have a chance—that's if he can get her to quit dodging him at every turn. The woman was going to be his, whether or not she knew it.

Dr. Mackenzie "Mac" Minton not once has regretted the decision to change her field of study from trauma surgeon to obstetrics and gynecology—only what caused her to make the choice.

Now in a town she'd visited as a child with her OBGYN practice specializing in high-risk pregnancies, she is content. At least in her professional life. Her personal life—a totally different subject. And Mac's not sure she'll ever find contentment there. However, she is certain the larger than life, and an overbearing biker is definitely not the answer to her problem.

Well, mostly certain.

Table of Contents

Prologue

Coast

I leaned against the clubhouse and watched the doctor dance with every brother who asked her. I wanted her in my arms, my bed, and my name echoing off the walls when I brought her to completion. It was her I wanted under me when my release took my breath, and my heart pounded in my chest.

Mackenzie avoided me at all costs since the day at the diner when I snapped at her about paying for lunch. I hadn't known then what made me do it, but now, as I watched her head lean back while she laughed at something Bull said, it was because she could destroy me. I knew it the minute she walked out of her office building that day, and I'd laid eyes on her for the first time. So, I made a play for her. Even now, knowing she could crush me, I would not be able to stay away from her much longer.

I lost sight of Mac when the music stopped, and River and Jag moved to the front of everyone.

"You boys are falling quickly. It's been a long time since the clubhouse hosted a wedding celebration. Hell, I think it was when Dare married Shakes."

I glanced over at my dad as he leaned against the building beside me, then I turned back to watch River as she prepared to toss her flowers to the women who had formed a group.

"I figure we'll see a few more before long. Maybe we can get the others to do it at the same time," I said, and my dad, Cruz, chuckled.

"Damn, I hope we don't have to break up a bunch of women fighting over flowers." I shook my head at my dad's comment and watched the group of women laugh as they moved around each other to get into the best position.

"Thelma's in the group. You not worried she might catch it?" I cocked my brow at my dad when he turned his head toward me.

"You got something to ask me, Emery?"

"Nope, so don't get your back bent all out of shape. But Bull and Tank might think differently."

"I'll speak with them if the need arises. Neither she nor I need your boys' permission. But out of respect for them as members of this club and Thelma's sons, I'll speak with them." I grinned at my dad. "What?"

"Doesn't seem like 'us boys' are the only ones falling quickly. What happened to the *We're going to do what we want, when we want, and enjoy taking off on our bikes whenever the road calls to us,*' speech?"

"We still can. It just means a warm woman behind me on the bike and in the bed at night."

"Christ, Dad, you might not want to make that comment when you talk to Bull and Tank."

"I might be older, Emery, but I have lost none of my brain function. And I plan to keep it that way."

"Yeah, it isn't your brain I'm worried about, Dad. Now, your ability to move around after they get a hold of you—a whole different thing."

"You're such a fucking smartass," my dad said and chuckled.

Loud laughter and squeals ended our conversation and had us looking toward the women just in time to watch the bundle of flowers arch and then disappear into the middle of the group. When the crowd separated, a grin split my face when I saw the flowers in Mac's hands.

"She's a tough little thing to have gotten in there and come out the victor. Not bad on the eyes either, huh? You know, tradition would have her as the next bride. Be interesting to see who snags the garter."

I glanced at my dad and didn't miss the smirk on his face. "What the hell does one have to do with the other?"

"See, that's what's wrong with today's world. Young people don't give a shit about traditions. You'd think having knowledge at their fingertips with the internet and the search engines, their intelligence would be advanced to a whole new level. No, instead, everything offends them and then they need time off because of it. Don't even get me started on trophies for participation."

"Really? I had no clue my dad was a stickler for wedding traditions, and an analyst for the problems with today's youth," I said to get my dad away from the subject of Mac, and maybe because I enjoyed getting him going. It took little to send the man into a tangent. I laughed when he smacked my stomach with the back of his hand.

"You've always been mouthy. What can I say? I know a lot of shit. Granted, some is useful, and some just takes up space in my head." We both chuckled, then my dad continued. The more he talked, the more my grin spread.

"You know, I might be able to work with that," I said. The information my dad shared appealed to me. If nothing else, it'd give me an opportunity to touch Mac.

"I thought you might find it interesting." My dad winked. "And perfect timing for it, too," he added with a chin lift. When I followed the direction he pointed toward, I watched the women set a chair down, then wave River over to stand beside it. They pointed to where they wanted the men, who stood nearby, to move.

I pushed off the wall of the clubhouse. "Thanks for the chat, old man. And the information," I said as I placed a hand on his neck and planted a kiss on his forehead, then released him.

"What the hell was that for, Emery?"

"Everything you've ever done for me." I turned to leave when his hand landed on my shoulder. I turned my head to the side and glanced over my shoulder at him.

"Son, you'll always be the best thing to have happened in my life. Never forget that."

I stared at my dad, then placed my hand on top of his and squeezed. "I think that's my line. You've always been there for me, no matter what. Even when you may have disagreed with my choices or a decision I made. I hope you know it goes both ways. You decide to pursue Thelma, then I'm in your corner. And I'll have your back if Bull and Tank give you shit over it."

When I let go of his hand, he removed his from my shoulder and slapped my back. "Go join the others before we get any mushier."

"But I love ya, old man," I said, grinning over my shoulder as I walked away.

"Love you, son."

I was still smiling as I walked toward the grumbling and complaining group of men.

"I give this party fifteen minutes after the kids are taken home to get out of hand. Two-thirds of the brothers are already drunk off their asses," Flirt said as I moved to stand beside him while he waved his hand in front of us to the group of unattached brothers the women had gathered. Most of them swayed on their feet as they grumbled. Though I found it amusing that not one of them moved from where the women told them to stand.

13

"It will be good as long as they don't make any fast moves. Otherwise, we could be untangling them for days," I said as Bull grabbed the back of Tank's vest when he tilted forward.

"Damn women, I didn't want any part of this either." Flirt pointed to Carly, Sami, Bailey, and Luna as they stood in front of the group. "'*Oh, just do it. He's your brother. It's his and River's day.*' That was Carly's speech, then Sami's and Luna's eyes watered up. Because pregnancy hormones are a bitch. Then Speed and Ghost glared at me as if daring me to hurt the women's feelings. Bailey, she didn't say a word, just pointed to where I needed to go. So yeah, here I am with these drunk bastards, wondering when we lost our dicks and grew vaginas."

I snorted and wondered how much Flirt had drank.

"Yet, you're standing here bitching like a woman," Ghost said as he walked up and smacked Flirt on the back. I snorted when Flirt flipped him off.

"Fuck you, Ghost. You're only saying that because I didn't hear them harassing you or the others into this crap. A matter of fact, after the women got their way and corralled us, your asses scattered," Flirt griped.

"Hey, it's for unattached brothers, which we are not. But I'm not ashamed to admit that goddamn straight we got the hell away. And I plan to keep away from the women in case they change their minds. Devil mentioned that he, Crusher, Speed, and I needed to restock the bar and coolers before the after-the-kids-hour party gets underway." Ghost chuckled and started toward the clubhouse. Where I would

14

guarantee the others were already hiding since they were nowhere in sight as I glanced around the yard.

"Sad day when bikers hide from a group of women!" I yelled.

Ghost never missing a step as he yelled over his shoulder. "Being a biker ain't got shit to do with it. Having smokin' hot sex later because our women are feeling all romantic and shit—everything."

Flirt and I laughed and watched Ghost make a beeline for the backdoor of the clubhouse.

"He's come a long way since you brought him home with you, Flirt." I shook my head as we watched Ghost stop at the backdoor and look around before he slipped into the clubhouse.

"I'm not going to lie. There were days I wondered if my old friend would ever reappear. I knew he was struggling, and it sucked ass not being able to help him. Running into Luna couldn't have come at a better time for him. Don't know how much longer he would have lasted if she hadn't come back into his life."

"Can't deny our brothers are proof of what a good woman can do for you," I said while I looked around for Mac and saw her standing off to the side.

"If you see that, then what the fuck are you waiting for, Coast? You've never held back when you wanted something. I'm not understanding why you're holding off now. Especially if you can have the chance at what the others have found."

The whistles and catcalls had Flirt and me facing toward the front of the crowd where River sat in the chair, and Jag kneeled in front of her. The sounds resulted because her dress slid halfway up her thigh when Jag lifted one of her legs and rested her foot on his shoulder.

We watched our brother as he ran his hands from River's ankle and up her leg until he reached the garter she wore around mid-thigh. He popped the band but left it where it was and ran his hands back down her leg. Boos erupted, and Jag turned toward the crowd and smirked, then turned back, placed his lips at River's ankle, and kissed and nibble his way up her leg.

"Good grief, I'm going inside until this is over. One investigation in a man's career is plenty," Sheriff Lance mumbled as he moved past Flirt and me. We waited until he was out of earshot before we laughed.

"I hope to hell he isn't packing. Things could get out of hand."

"Jag's safe. Will actually likes him. And I don't think the investigation bothered him as much as the ex-son-in-law still breathing does. That pisses him off more than anything," I said as hoots and hollers filled the air and grew louder as River blushed and covered her face with her hands.

"Yeah, and it wouldn't look good to kill his grandbaby's daddy."

"There is that," I answered as Jag's mouth reached the garter on River's thigh. He used his teeth to grab hold of it, then worked it down River's leg until he had it off. After he pulled her hands from her face and kissed her on the lips, he stood.

"You know, sometimes I don't give my dad enough credit," I said, and Flirt looked at me, and furrowed his brows.

"For what?" Just as Flirt asked, Jag used the pointer finger on each of his hands and launched the garter slingshot style into the air.

"Reminding me some traditions are important to keep up with." I chuckled as I watched my brothers shove each other around.

"What the hell are you talking about, Coast?" Flirt asked as we continued to watch the pushing and shoving going on.

"That both sides of me are full of superstitions and traditions." The garter began to fall, and I stepped into the middle of the fray, raised my arm, and used my hand to snatch it out of the air. When I pulled back and stood with the garter in my hand, Flirt shook his head.

"What's gotten into you, brother?" Flirt looked at me as if I'd lost my damn mind.

Honestly, maybe I had, because most men would walk away if a woman dodged them as often as Mac had done to me the last few months.

"Working on a strategy," I answered while I looked around until I spotted Mac where she stood with the other women and clapped as Jag lifted River up and carried her off.

Flirt and I were silent as we watched the couple stop where Flyboy, Jag's dad, stood with Poppy in his arms. Jag's baby girl's giggles when Jag leaned in and kissed all over her small face had me smiling.

"How soon do you think it will take before Flyboy is calling Shakes or one of the other women to help with Pop?" Flirt asked while we continued to watch the interaction between Jag and his daughter before he led River toward the road to our houses. They were spending the night on the compound, then leaving in the morning for a few days away before River started her teaching job at the school.

"The dads handled us as kids. I think Flyboy can take care of one little girl," I said while I focused my eyes back on the woman who had held my attention for months.

"You're right, but we've learned with Ally and Neely that girls are way different than boys," Flirt countered.

"Brother, you have issues if it took you that long to realize they're different," I smirked while Flirt glared.

"Hilarious. Now let's get back to you realizing both sides of your bloodline follow various traditions. From my perspective, it sounds to me like you might finally have found your balls, brother," Flirt said and slapped my shoulder.

"I never lost them. It took a bit for me to remember that patience was never my strong point."

Flirt's laughter followed me as I started closing the distance between myself and what I wanted.

Mac.

Mac looked up at me when I stopped in front of her. Then she frowned when I squatted down.

"You're going to want to hold on to my shoulders, Mac." Without waiting for her to comply, I grabbed one of her legs and lifted it, which left her no choice but to grab hold of my shoulders if she wanted to keep her balance.

"Umm, damn," Luna said.

Sami followed with, "Holy shit."

"What are you doing, Emery?" Mac asked as I slid the garter over her shoe. "Oh my God, stop gawking and help me."

I would have chuckled at the desperate plea toward the women if I hadn't had to concentrate on the task of slipping the garter on her. And I hadn't thought how touching her skin intimately would affect me as much as her, either. Not to mention the subtleness of her perfume wrapping around me.

"Mackenzie, you've been around the men enough to know they don't follow orders well," Carly said and chuckled.

I grinned as I glanced up and saw Mac glaring at Carly, then she looked at Bailey. "Really? A friend, plus you work for me?"

"Yes, and you can thank me later for not interfering." Bailey winked at me, and I grinned when Mac mumbled "traitor."

"Well, I think it would be a good time for us to find our men," Carly said, and the other women agreed.

"I can't believe you are deserting me," Mac said, sounding a little disgruntled, which made my grin broaden.

She huffed when Luna said, "You look like you're in quite capable hands."

"I agree. Let's go find our men," Bailey said and grabbed Luna's elbow and led her away.

I knew it was wrong, but the women were helping me out, so I said over my shoulder, "You'll find your men in the clubhouse—hiding out." The women grumbled and headed in the clubhouse's direction.

That would teach the assholes.

"I can't believe you threw your friends under the—" Mac never finished her sentence when I started slowly sliding the band up her leg.

The feel of her smooth skin under my hands had me biting back a groan. I wanted to place her off balance, and the shiver that ran through her body and the change in the tone of her voice let me know I succeeded.

"Emery," Mac said breathlessly as I paused at her knee and caressed the tender skin behind before I moved the garter over the small cap of her knee.

"You only have to tell me to stop, *cariño*," I lowered my voice and looked up at Mac when no reply came. "But I really hope you don't."

Once my hands reached the middle of her thigh, I stopped and released the garter. I felt the heat radiating from her core and with my large hand on her inner thigh, my fingertips touched the material of her panties. I wanted nothing more than to push the material aside and slide my fingers through her warmth and let the heat of her engulf them. Instead, I pulled my hands away, sat her foot on the

20

ground, and straightened her dress where my actions had pushed the hem up. Then I stood.

"Dance with me, *cariño?*" I asked and held my hand out.

Mac paused a moment. "What's all this about, Emery?" she asked as she placed her hand in mine.

"Do you know the belief behind the garter being placed on the woman who catches the bouquet?"

"Seriously, you're interested in wedding traditions?" The way Mac's brows furrowed and the intense way she stared me in the eyes, I wouldn't have been surprised if I saw gears moving. She was trying to figure me out, and it wasn't working well for her.

"So, do you know or not?" I pressed.

"Ugh, are you telling me you honestly believe the woman who catches the bouquet becomes the next to marry? Then yes, who hasn't heard that tale?"

"It isn't only about the woman who catches the bouquet. The man who catches the garter will be the one she marries." I kept my face blank as I looked down at her.

"How much have you had to drink? You're acting strange, even for you."

I hadn't been able to keep my lips from twitching. The woman had no clue. The more she pushed me, the more I'd push back.

"Considering you run in the other direction when you see me. How would you know how I act? Have you been watching me, Mac, when I'm not looking?"

She tried to pull her hand from mine, but I tightened my grip and wouldn't allow it.

"One experience with your arrogance was enough. Why would I want to come back for more?"

"Just once, if you would've given me a chance before you took off in the opposite direction, you might've been shocked and received an apology. I'll admit my reaction to your offer to pay for lunch in the diner that day was a bit—"

"Over the top. Dickish. Assholish. Being a big jer…"

"I wouldn't go that far, Doc."

"Oh, now I'm doc and not sweetheart, love, honey, or baby. But I guess it beats bitch."

I could not keep the grin off my face. "Understand Spanish, do you? And for the record, I've never called you a bitch. What I said to you that day was to stop bitching, or I was going to turn you over my knee and spank your ass. Which I might still do if you don't stop glaring at me as if you're trying to make me burst into flames."

"*Entender y hablar un poco de español, idiota*! I understand and speak some Spanish, idiot. And you wouldn't dare spank me," Mac said defiantly.

"Oh, but I would, *cariño*. Then I'd kiss those cheeks before fucking you until we both passed out."

"Oh my God, you're too much. I apologize for calling you an idiot. But damn it, you piss me. One minute you're pulling a garter up my thigh, talking some nonsense about marriage traditions, calling me sweetheart in Spanish, then you're talking about what you're going to do to me," Mac said and looked around, I assumed to see if anyone had overheard as we stopped at the edge of the makeshift dance floor. "What do you want from me, Emery?"

"That's a loaded question. Come on, Mac, let's start with a dance." The current song was ending, and I moved us into the middle of the group still dancing, before she had time to react.

When *Slow Hands* by Niall Horan started, Mac reached up and placed her hands around my neck, and I wrapped my arms around her waist and pulled her close into my body for the slow song. With my height and bulk compared to her small stature, we shouldn't work, but we did. She felt right in my arms.

"No one can predict the future," I said offhandedly as I breathed her in.

"Huh?"

No way was I going to explain to her that my thoughts were stuck on if there was any truth in the old wives' tale of the bouquet and garter toss recipients marrying. Instead, I answered, "Nothing. Listen. Feel."

As we rocked and swayed, I leaned my head down until my face rested in the crook of Mac's neck. Her hair was pulled up into some kind of twist that left her neck exposed, and I planned to take full advantage. With the lightest of touches, I ran my lips up her soft skin until I reached her ear. When my lips closed over the lobe of her ear, I bit gently and sucked. Mac moaned softly, and her body melted more into mine.

The taste of her, the smell, everything about her had me as lost in her as she was in me. The fingertips of her hands skimmed my neck, touched, then ran through my hair over and over.

As the song played, I whispered some lyrics to her as my hands traveled up and down the skin of her back, left bare from the dress she wore. There was just the two of us, and nothing around us mattered. I wanted every word in the song to be about us. And I most certainly had no intention of leaving without her on me, as the song words say.

"Come home with me, Mac. I want your naked body wrapped around me. I want to feel us skin against skin. I want to taste every inch of you, feel the heat as I enter you and take us both up and over the edge. Then I want to do it all again."

"Oh God, Emery."

"Say yes, Mac. Let me take you and bring you to orgasm until you're gasping for breath and hoarse from screaming my name."

I kissed down her neck, across her collarbone while my hands traveled to her waist and up until my thumbs touched and caressed the outer curve of her breasts. I nibbled her chin as I made my way to her mouth, sucked her bottom lip between my teeth and bit down gently, only to slide my tongue across to take away the sting.

"Emery, please—" Mackenzie stopped talking as a chime came from a phone.

"Don't answer it," I said and captured her lips. When my tongue pushed through, she groaned, and as quick as the kiss started, it ended.

Mac leaned away just enough to shove her hand into the 'V' of her dress. When she brought her hand out, it held a ringing cellphone. She looked at the screen, and after a swipe of her thumb, she moved the phone to her ear.

"Dr. Minton," Mac answered as I released her from my arms and maneuvered us out of the crowd. Our moment broken.

A man's voice could be heard, but I couldn't make out what he said. I stopped us at the far end of the clubhouse away from the speakers blasting the music.

"That's great, Neal. Yes, there's no need to panic, you got this. Sarah will be fine. Just keep thinking that when it's over, you will get to hold your son. I'll meet you at the hospital, Daddy. And don't forget to put mom in the car." Mac chuckled, then smiled at whatever the man replied before she disconnected the call. "I've got to go."

"I heard."

"I'm sorry. I... I—"

"Why? Because you have to do your job?"

"No, I... I'm not sure I can do this." She waved her hand between us. "And crap, I don't have time to discuss it right now. I need to leave."

"You've been running, and I don't understand why, but it stops. I want you, Mac, and I intend to have you. But I can wait a little longer."

"I don't know how long it will take. Sarah is a first time—"

"Mac!" I raised my voice to cut her off before she spiraled out of control, thinking about the possibility of us when she had a job to do.

"What?"

"Go deliver the baby. You and I will finish what we started sooner rather than later." When Mac opened her mouth to speak, I held up my hand. "I can stand here and watch you while you walk to your car and leave. Or I can walk you to your car, bend you over the hood, hike that little dress up, and—"

"I'm going," was the only thing Mac said as she turned and dashed toward her car.

I grinned and stood at the edge of the clubhouse until I lost sight of her taillights. Instead of going back to the party, I headed toward my place. I'd give her a couple of hours, then I would head to the hospital and wait for her. No matter how long the delivery took.

The feeling of contentment was with me as I stepped into my house. As I closed the door, my phone rang, and I pulled it out of my pocket and glanced at the screen. I answered the call with the swipe of my thumb, but unlike Mac's call, I knew mine wasn't going to make me happy.

Chapter One

Coast

Riding across the tribal lands, I glanced around. The only light came from my lone headlight, or the occasional light shining in a resident's yard. Even under the cover of night, I knew I passed areas where the housing was nothing more than hovels lined up. Poverty ran high on the reservation. And it wasn't the first time I rode through and was thankful my dad had fought for me.

If I'd grown up on the reservation, I knew in my heart I would have either ended up in prison as my mom's dad had, who eventually died after being shanked in the prison yard. Or I would have died from an overdose like my mom had and her mother before her.

I'd visited the reservation at least twice a year since I turned two. At first, my dad would bring me and stay. By the time I reached my teens, he would drop me off, then return for me a week later.

After I joined the military, my visits became far and few between depending on when I made it home on leave. Since leaving the military, I'd only visited twice and stayed for only a couple of days each time.

Within an hour of receiving the call that hampered my plans of surprising Mac after Jag and River's wedding celebration, I packed a few things in my saddlebags, spoke with my dad, and was on the road. Dealing with Mac would have to wait.

The ride to the reservation had only taken me a few hours, but the miles had been lonely. Both my dad and Flirt had volunteered to make the trip with me, but I declined the offers. I needed the alone time on my bike to work through the feelings I held for Mac. Wanting her was easy. And I knew I could get her in my bed, it was keeping her there. I wanted what my brothers had found with their women. In my heart, I knew Mac belonged to me. Convincing her I was her one would be the test of my patience. One test I had no plans of failing.

The closer I got to my great grandfather's place, the more ashamed of myself I became. Kiyaya Young was the only person from my maternal side who still lived. He was one of the few people who gave a shit that I existed. I owed him more than the occasional visit. He was the only reason I visited the reservation. Because of him, I had the knowledge of my ancestry, spoke some of the Sahaptin dialect, and understood tribal life. He was smart, stubborn, and a hardass.

And he'd be mad as hell when I showed up on his doorstep. Thinking about his reaction made me smile.

When I rode up to Kiyaya's small wooden home, I no sooner shut my bike down, and a low wattage light on the porch turned on, followed by the front door being opened. My great grandfather's form filled the doorway. He was one hundred percent Native American and looked every bit the part of an aging warrior.

At eighty-nine, his hair was white, and his face was covered in weathered skin. I knew if I saw him from behind, his braided ponytail would reach the middle of his back. If not for the weathered skin of his face and the white hair, most wouldn't be able to come close in guessing the man's age.

I dismounted my bike as he stepped out onto the porch. He was tall and lean, and his expression was not one of a happy man.

"Goddamn, Suni. That woman needs to mind her own business," he said with half the words in English and the other half in his native language. When he combined the two languages, it was a definite sign he was pissed.

So, of course, I responded with a smile on my face, "Eh, nice to see you, too, old man."

"Ain't you got better shit to do than to come here to harass me? It's time you found a woman. Settled down and had a few kids."

I chuckled and grabbed my saddlebags. "Who says I don't have a woman? I haven't been here in eight months.

Besides, do you think it's a good idea for you to be outside?" I asked as I made my way toward the porch.

He huffed and turned around and went inside. I followed and shut the door behind me.

"Do you have a *áyat*?" he asked as he walked to the stove.

"No, I don't have a woman. Yet. I'm working on it."

"What's there to work on? You find an *áyat*, then you make her yours." He poured heated water into a cup and stirred it before turning and setting it on the table.

"Is that how you caught Aahna?"

He smiled, then started coughing. I walked to him and pulled a chair out and helped him to sit. After the coughing spell was over and he'd taken a drink of whatever was in his cup, he answered, "Your great grandmother was a strong and beautiful woman. Many tried to gain her attention. It had been my honor to have been chosen by her. A man needs a strong *ásham*, by his side."

"I can't argue with that. But you sure when from having a woman to a wife damn quick," I said, chuckling as I moved to the other side of the open area toward the door to the second bedroom.

"Why would you argue? I am right."

I shook my head and snorted, "What are you doing up so late?"

"Fixin' tea. Can't sleep for the coughing."

I dropped the bags by the door that led into the second bedroom, then pulled my gloves off and stuffed them in the pockets of my jacket before I slipped it off and hung it on the doorknob.

The wooden home had two small bedrooms, a bathroom, and one open area that had the kitchen on one side and the living room on the other. I looked around, and nothing had changed since the last time I had been there.

"Damn, no wonder you're sick. It's fucking cold in here." I glanced at the wood-burning stove in the corner that should have been in use but wasn't. "Is there a reason you're not burning the stove?"

"Ran out of chopped wood this morning and wasn't up to cutting any."

"There are enough unemployed fuckers around here that would gladly chop some wood for a few bucks," I said as I reached for my jacket.

"Why should I waste money paying someone when I can do it myself?" he asked, then broke out coughing.

I pulled my jacket back on and rolled my eyes. "Because you are sick. Suni is worried about you," I answered and moved toward the back door.

"She worries too much. I have a cold. That's all." I looked over my shoulder and lifted a brow. "Grab the *lakayxit'áwas* (lantern) on the counter. The light on the back porch doesn't work."

I was ready with a remark about him being stubborn, but his last words stopped me. How many more things needed to be fixed around his home?

Oh, I'd fix a few things when I blew through; a leaky faucet, a board on a porch step if I felt it give. I'd even stock

31

him up with nonperishable supplies, then be on my way. Not for the first time, I felt shame. I said he was the only family I had left from my maternal side without a thought to being his *only* family.

Born and raised on the reservation, Kiyaya would never leave, but it didn't mean I couldn't be a better grandson.

He stood as I grabbed the lantern off the counter. "I think I'm going to lie down. I'm tired."

I nodded, opened the door, and stepped out, pulling it closed behind me. Once the lantern was lit, I walked to the woodpile and positioned the lantern for optimum light. Then I jerked the axe out of the log and started splitting the wood. Nothing like physical labor to clear my head.

As the chopped woodpile grew, the more things became apparent. I'd wasted good energy on despising a mother who'd had no interest in me from the time I was conceived. Drugs and alcohol had been her top priorities. If not for my dad making her stick around the club and keeping her away from drugs and alcohol until I was born, who knew what would have happened to me.

After I was born, Aponi, my mother, turned me over to my dad and hightailed it back to the reservation. The place she'd run away from looking for something better. I hadn't realized how much energy I'd wasted on a woman who died before I reached the age of two. It was long past the time to kick her out of my head. I'd spent far too much of my life carrying the burden of not being enough of a reason for her to stay clean.

I stuck the axe back in the log, loaded my arms with enough wood to start the stove, and headed back to the house. Once the stove was stoked and heat filled the room, I headed to the bedroom. When I rested my head on the pillow and closed my eyes, exhaustion took me under.

The front door opened, then closed on my great grandfather's house while I sat in one of the two chairs on the small front porch. Suni White, one of the tribe's elders and the one who called me the day before, held out a mug in front of me.

"He's resting," Suni said as I reached for the mug. She then sat in the chair beside me.

"How long has he been sick?"

"Ah, you know Kiyaya. He keeps to himself and doesn't want to be a burden to anyone. His stubborn streak has always been wide. I stopped by last week to check in on him. He was coughing, and I could hear rattling in his chest. I offered to take him to the clinic, but he refused and argued with me. The more I pushed, the more upset he became, and then he went into a coughing fit, so I dropped it. He told me he was using his own medicines."

I rubbed my hand down my face, leaned forward, and rested my elbows on my knees, holding the cup between my hands. "Yeah, because a few herbs in a burlap pouch laying on his chest or herbs boiled into tea is the cure-all. Let's not forget to add the burning of incense to the list of remedies. I woke to the smell of the damn incense after only four hours of sleep. Hell, it might not cure him, but he'd feel better if he

33

ground those damn leaves and mixed them into a glass of Jack Daniels."

Suni chuckled. "Now you know why I called, Emery."

I turned my head and looked at the older woman. Her face wrinkled with age. Her long gray hair pulled back in a braid that fell down her back. Suni's dark brown eyes stared back at me, and they held knowledge, wisdom, truth, and compassion in their depths.

As a respected elder in the Yakama tribe, Suni was one of the few who always attempted to visit me when I came to my great grandfather's home over the years. She was also one of the few who'd joined my great grandfather and taken my dad's side against the council that thought it best if I was raised on the reservation. The council wanted me to be in touch with the culture of my half Native American blood.

"Oh, so I get to be the bad guy."

Suni threw her head back and laughed in earnest, then sobered and faced me once more. "Your visits to the reservation were always looked forward to, Emery. Kiyaya would tell anyone who would listen to you coming for a visit. He has always been proud of you and your accomplishments. When I gave support to Emilo after finding out Aponi had given birth to you, I wondered if I would regret going along with Kiyaya's wishes. Watching you grow up was proof my decision had been right. You've turned into quite a good man."

As I sat and listened to Suni talk about standing beside my great grandfather against the council, which they were both a part of back then, it wasn't the first time I wondered if there hadn't been more between her and Kiyaya other than friends.

Suni White had never been married or had children of her own. She'd grown up on the reservation and been best friends with my great grandmother, who had passed away when Aponi, my mother, had been in her teens.

She and Kiyaya were raising their granddaughter, Aponi, at the time because their daughter-in-law had died from an overdose when my mother had been only three months old. Funny how history seemed to repeat itself. Aponi had done the same with me. Two years after Aponi's mother overdosed, Aponi's father, Kiyaya's son and my grandfather, was sent to prison for life after he'd stabbed a man in a bar fight, then beat the man within an inch of his life. Leaving my mother to live with her grandparents.

"Thanks, but not that good of a man. I could've done more for Kiyaya over the years, Suni." When Suni arrived that morning to look in on Kiyaya, I used the opportunity to take a really good look around the house. Some things needed to be repaired, like the roof and the doors needed new weather-stripping. The windows had plastic on them, and I still felt the cold seeping in. They needed replaced.

"Eh, that is you thinking he would have allowed it. Kiyaya is a stubborn man, Emery."

"I could have tried. Done better by him. And since I can't go back and change the past, I'll just have to do better going forward. Starting with fixing some things around this place. But first, he needs to go to the clinic. What I heard last night and this morning with his cough, I wouldn't be

35

surprised if he doesn't have bronchitis. Or worse, pneumonia. And if that's the case, his medicine pouches aren't going to cut it."

Suni smiled. "Maybe start with your concern to get him to agree to go to the clinic instead of mentioning his medicines."

I drank the last of my coffee and stood. "I might if I was going to ask him."

Suni stuck out her hand, and I took hold, helping her out of the chair. Once she stood, she squeezed my forearm. "I'm glad you came."

"Great, then you can stand up for me when he calls the cops to toss my ass off the reservation's land."

"Eh, it will be okay." Suni patted my arm as we moved to the door. "I know the chief's mother."

I chuckled. "Well, in that case, what are we waiting for?" I opened the door. "No time like the present."

Chapter Two

Mac

After hanging my jacket on the rack in the corner of my office, I stretched, then walked to my desk and picked up the Styrofoam cup of coffee I snagged before leaving the hospital. I took a drink and set the cup back down as Bailey stuck her head in the open door.

"Morning. I have the exam rooms ready," she said and walked into my office.

"Good morning, and thanks," I said as I pulled out my chair and plopped down.

"Geez, did you spend the weekend at the hospital?" Bailey asked as she sat in the chair on the other side of my desk.

I looked down at the scrubs I wore with the hospital logo on them. "I did."

"Did you get to go home at all after you left River and Jag's reception?"

"No. I went straight to the hospital to deliver the Michaelson's baby, and before Sarah delivered, the Nelson's and the Moore's showed up." I grinned. "Two girls and one boy in a little over thirty-six hours."

"Holy crap, did you get any sleep?"

"A few hours here and there in the doctor's lounge between deliveries. At least I was able to grab a shower before I came here this morning." I held up my cup of coffee. "This has kept me going."

"Well, that isn't good. We'll go to the diner when we close for lunch," Bailey said and stood. "Because I know you hate the cafeteria food and probably ate out of the vending machines."

"You know me so well." I rubbed my stomach. "The diner sounds good. I'd kill for a double cheeseburger, fries, and a chocolate milkshake."

Bailey chuckled and shook her head. "Just the thought of that, and I can feel my thighs and butt enlarging."

"As long as you don't overindulge, you can eat whatever you have a craving for," I told her as I pushed my chair back and stood.

"Says the woman who eats as much as any man and never gains a pound," Bailey sneered.

"Please, like," I waved my hand from my breasts to my feet, "you'd want this body. Besides, Devil would love you no matter if you gained five hundred pounds. Pregnancy suits you. You're practically glowing."

Bailey grinned, then chuckled. "Oh, I know someone who wants your body."

I put my hand up. "Don't even go there. I'm still mad at you for abandoning me with him."

"Oh, come on, Mackenzie. Everyone around witnessed the chemistry between you and Emery. He's been after you since the day in the diner. You just avoid him," Bailey said, then her eyebrows furrowed, and she moved to the door, pushing it closed before she looked back at me. "It isn't because he's half Mexican and half Native American, is it?"

I wasn't sure which feeling was stronger: the hurt because she thought Emery's ethnicity mattered or the anger because she thought he's ethnicity was a factor to me staying away from him.

"Oh my God, Bailey, I can't believe you asked that. You seriously can't think that matters to me. Do you?"

"No, but I had to be sure. Coast... You know, I was a few years behind all the guys in school and they were friends with my brother, James?" I nodded, and Bailey continued. "Shades Valley has a lot of wonderful people and a lot of *not* so wonderful people. They're folks who hate having the MC here, even though they've been around forever. So being a part of the MC and then mixed on top of it made Coast an easy target in school for the kids who were..."

"Bigots, assholes, racists." I knew my voice rose with each word, but I was raised by parents who taught my brother and me you treated everyone with the same respect you yourself demanded. Their color, their age, their sex, their religion, their politics, or whether they were rich or poor, didn't matter. My dad had said nobody had a right to judge another person because you've never walked in their shoes, lived with their struggles, or witnessed firsthand anything to do with their lives.

As a young girl, I hadn't comprehended some of the things he said, but as I'd grown older, they'd become much clearer. How much better off would humanity be if everyone looked beyond the appearance of a person? Or if they didn't get bent out of shape because someone else acted differently or didn't share the same views? How boring would the world be if we all looked or thought alike?

"Yeah, you're right on all accounts, Mac."

"After meeting Emery and the other men, I can't imagine who would have the balls to bully Emery."

"Well, he wasn't always as big as he is now, but it wasn't so much as pushing him around as it was the snide comments and slurs as he passed by. It happened mostly when he was alone. If the others heard anyone make a comment, there was hell to pay, and it involved getting bloody. But it wasn't only the boys in school, it was the girls."

"Why? Let me guess. Because he didn't pay them any attention?" I knew girls could be mean, but it was mostly toward other girls.

"Umm… no. The bitches drooled over him. Hell, they drooled over them all. Being part of the MC alone made them appealing to the twats. Add in their looks and it was like toss a piece of raw meat into a shark tank."

"Ah, they wanted bragging rights," I said as I draped my stethoscope around my neck.

"Exactly. So, it was hard to tell who legitimately liked him or just wanted to use him to make their daddy mad. Now don't get me wrong, Coast had no issue accepting what they offered, but it made him... for lack of a better word, harder. More cautious about who he trusts and lets get close to him. What I've gotten from overhearing the men talk about their time in the military, it wasn't much different for Coast there either," Bailey finished and opened the door as I walked toward her.

"I'm not avoiding Emery because of his race, Bailey."

"I'm sorry I jumped to that conclusion. But, Mac, if you really aren't interested in him, be upfront. He'll back off."

"Really, he'll back off?" I cocked an eyebrow at Bailey.

"Okay, okay." Bailey put her hands up and grinned. "Probably not. More like he'll turn the pressure up a notch to convince you. If you haven't noticed, the men are a tad pushy."

I laughed. "Pushy. Don't you mean arrogant, bossy, controlling?"

Bailey patted my arm as we headed out of the office. "See, you understand them. You'll fit right into club life."

"Whoa, girlfriend. You are getting way ahead of yourself. I don't even know Emery that well."

"Whose fault is that?"

I hooked my arm through Bailey's as we walked to the first exam room. "You know, I think the men are rubbing off on you," I said, releasing Bailey as I reached for the chart in the box beside the exam room's door.

"No, I think it's the baby. It's taken my filter away."

I was chuckling as I entered the exam room to start the day. My earlier exhaustion forgotten.

I walked out of one exam room and headed across the hall to another. One more appointment left and then lunch. As I reached for the chart, my stomach rumbled, and I rubbed it. I opened the chart and smiled at the name. I'd forgotten they were on the schedule for today.

"How are you both today?" I asked as I walked into the exam room where Sami was lying on the table while Speed stood beside her.

"Excited," Sami said as Speed gave me a chin lift.

I walked to the counter and grabbed a pair of gloves, pulling them on. "Your weight and vitals couldn't be any better. Are you still experiencing morning sickness?"

"No, thank goodness. I was tiring of hugging the toilet first thing after my feet hit the floor in the morning."

"Good to hear. You're into your second trimester, and it usually subsides by then. Everything seems to be progressing normally, so let's get to it and see if the little one cooperates this time around with the sonogram." I grabbed and rolled the machine closer to the table, angling it so the three of us could watch the screen. The first sonogram I'd given Sami, the baby refused to cooperate, keeping its legs bent and together.

I squeezed the gel onto Sami's belly, then grabbed the device and began sliding it across her stomach as I focused on the screen. Everything looked excellent with the little one, and today it had decided not to be shy.

Once I turned the dial on the machine, the room filled with the sound of the baby's heartbeat, and Kane leaned closer, squinting at the screen.

"Holy shit, most men would be damn proud to show that off. Don't know why he was shy the first time."

I couldn't keep the chuckle contained when Sami slapped Speed's forearm.

"Seriously, Kane? That is the first thing you notice? How do you even know you're looking at a winkie? It could be a leg."

"Well, then the kid has three of them," Speed said, but then glance toward me.

I smiled. "You're correct. It would be a penis," I answered, then hit the button to print a picture of the baby for them.

"Oh my God, a boy. Ally is going to be upset she's not getting a sister," Sami said, and Speed took his eyes off the screen and looked at Sami.

"My girl's tough. She'll survive," he said, then leaned down and kissed Sami, running his hand over the top of her head. "Love you, babe."

I turned away and took measurements of the little guy to give them their private moment. I loved my job and had no regrets about my choice of switching from trauma to OB and specializing in high-risk pregnancies. But there were times, like now, watching a couple's joy reminded me I'd never experience that feeling firsthand.

The tap on the door had me glancing over my shoulder, and as the door opened, Bailey's head popped in. "Well?"

I grinned, and Sami and Speed chuckled. "Couldn't take the suspense?" I asked as Bailey walked into the room.

"No. I tried to stay busy, but it was killing me."

"Because you're nosy."

My eyes widened, and I looked over at Speed, and his lips twitched.

"Shut up, Speed," Bailey said, then looked at the screen. "It's a boy!"

"See, babe. He is impressing the ladies already," Speed said, and Sami rolled her eyes.

I ran a towel over Sami's stomach to remove the gel, then handed her a towel to wipe any remaining I might have missed.

"You realize as he grows, it will look smaller compared to his body," I explained as I handed Speed the printout of the sonogram.

"Don't bother explaining, Mac. It won't do any good. Nor will it stop him from showing the pic to everyone we know," Sami said, and as she tried to push herself up, Speed hurriedly placed a hand behind her back to help.

"Hey, it's not just about the size of his dick. First boy in the group."

"There might be more boys depending what Luna's sonogram shows," Bailey said as she pushed the machine out of the way. "I'm surprised she hasn't tried to come in here."

"How did I not know Luna was on the schedule today, too?" I looked at Bailey.

"She's not. Her sonogram appointment is next week. She and Ghost came in to wait, and Lance stayed out in the truck with Ally and Neely. They're going to the diner for lunch, too."

"Yes, and we'll meet you there. Try not to take too long. I'm starved," Sami said as Speed help her off the table.

"You were the last appointment before lunch, so we'll only be a few minutes behind you," I said and reached for the door and pulled it open.

"Great. I'll show them out and let Amelia know she's clear to go to lunch also," Bailey said and followed Sami and Speed through the door.

"Thanks. I'll meet you out front after I swing by the office and grab my jacket and keys."

"Sounds good," Bailey answered, then walked away with Sami and Speed as I headed in the opposite direction toward my office.

Once inside, I grabbed my bag out of my desk and my jacket off the rack. No one mentioned Emery being outside or joining us at the diner, but it didn't keep me from getting that warm feeling in my stomach at the thought of being around him. For a brief second, I wondered if the exhaustion was back and influencing me.

I thought keeping my distance from the man would curb his interest and give me time to build up a resistance to him. And I had. At least until he pulled me against him to dance. Who was I kidding? He had my interest when he touched me to slide the garter up my leg. His fingers leaving a trail of fire on my skin. The dancing had only added to it.

The arrogance and bossy nature I could have dealt with, even ignored. It was the softer side of him that would be my downfall. I might not have had any intentions of getting involved, but I was grown up enough to admit it was too late.

"Ugh, I'm so damn screwed and not in a good way," I said into the empty hallway as I made way to the front.

Emery "Coast" Cortez had wormed his way under my skin when I wasn't looking. And I was not happy about it.

Chapter Three

Coast

"This is a waste of time. My medicines work fine." On the fifteen-minute drive to the clinic, Kiyaya had repeated the same words at least a hundred times.

I blew out a breath and opened the driver's side door on Kiyaya's thirty-year-old pickup. The rust was the only thing keeping the body of the truck together.

"Truck's about on its last leg."

"Nothing wrong with it. Young people always wanting new shiny things."

My lips twitched. Kiyaya had been arguing with everything I said since I informed him yesterday that he would be going to the clinic. Swinging my legs out, I got out of the truck and closed the door, then walked around the front and waited.

Kiyaya continued to sit in the passenger seat with his arms crossed and made no move to exit the vehicle. If the old man thought he could wait me out, he was in for a lesson. I had had enough the day before and told him he was going to the clinic if I had to drag his old ass. The only one amused by my great grandfather's ranting had been Suni. Then again, if I'd been the one getting to leave and not have to deal with him, I might have laughed as she had, too.

Instead, I spent the day fixing small things around his place: a leaky faucet, a clogged drain, and a few loose floorboards I found on both porches. I'd even chopped more wood and stacked it. Hell, I would have chopped more to stay outside, so I didn't have to listen to him gripe. As it was, there was enough wood until I made another trip back, which would be as soon as I could get the new windows and roofing supplies ordered and delivered to me. I would need a couple of my brothers to come along to help with the installation. The work that needed done was not a one-man job.

Leaning my butt against the hood, I bent one leg and propped my boot on the bumper and crossed my arms. Minutes ticked by, and several people entered and exited the clinic. I pulled my cell out and thumbed through my messages, and while I waited, I texted my dad, who texted back the laughing emoji when I'd texted what I was doing.

Finally, I heard the creak of the old truck's door, and when it shut, on a slam no less, I pushed off the front and stood on the sidewalk.

"Let's get it over with. I got things to do," Kiyaya said as he passed by me.

"The only thing you'll be doing is taking what medicines they prescribe and then resting." I reached in front of him and pulled the door open.

"I like it better when you only come two times a year," he mumbled as he walked in ahead of me.

I shook my head. "Go find a seat, and I'll check you in. If I'm lucky, they'll give you a shot in your ass using an enormous needle."

Kiyaya chuckled as he walked off, and I grinned as I reached the counter. After signing him in, I joined him in the seating area, taking a seat between him and a kid.

"I don't know why we have to be here," the kid next to me said to the woman on the other side of him, filling out paperwork.

"See, even the boy doesn't want to be here," Kiyaya said, and I leaned my head back against the wall and closed my eyes. I couldn't believe that less than forty-eight hours ago, I was holding Mac in my arms and working on getting her into my bed. Now, I sat with a crotchety old man, trying to get him to see a doctor.

"You know why we are here, Tracker. You and Paxton need to be checked out before we can place you with a foster family." I opened my eyes and looked over at the woman and noticed a younger boy sitting in the chair on the other side of her.

"Yeah, because you made us come."

Kiyaya snickered, and I cut my eyes to him. He shrugged. When I turned my head back, the woman was glaring at me, and the two boys were staring.

"You'll have to excuse him." I pointed with my thumb in Kiyaya's direction. "He isn't feeling well."

Christ, I was apologizing for a man pushing ninety. It was time I reevaluated my life.

"We're here 'cause our mom died," the younger boy said.

"Sorry for your loss," I said as an automatic response to hearing of someone's death.

"Why, you didn't know her?" The kid the woman called Tracker said, and the woman sighed.

"Tracker, that's enough," she said and looked at me apologetically.

"No, I didn't. But it doesn't mean I'm not sorry you and your brother lost your mother. It's called compassion."

"We lost her 'cause drugs were more important to her than us," Tracker said point blank while he looked directly in my eyes.

"Tracker—" the woman, who I assumed was a social worker, went to speak, and I gave a small shake of my head to cut her off.

I wasn't sure why I felt the need to talk with the kid. It could have been the look of defeat I saw in his eyes that he tried to cover up with attitude. Or hell, it could have been because I saw a little of myself in him. A glance at what I could have faced if my dad hadn't fought for me.

"Yeah, it sucks. But you can let her faults keep affecting you, or you can learn from her mistakes and want more out of life for you and your brother. Understand?"

"Easy for you to say. You don't have to live with strangers who only see you as a monthly check."

Damn, the kid was tough. "I could have been you, kid. But you're right, I didn't have to live with strangers because I had my dad. Your attitude isn't going to help you, though. Is it?" Tracker didn't respond, he just stared at me. I lifted my chin in his brother's direction. "He's going to follow your lead. You can either make the change easier for him or harder for both of you. Life's not fair, and you've learned that at an early age already, right?"

"I guess." Tracker broke eye contact and looked down at his lap and sighed as if in acceptance of the situation.

The sound grated on my nerves. I hated it. Who knew what the two boys had already been through and witnessed if their mom had been a drug addict?

I strongly needed to change the mood surrounding the kid. If only a temporary break from his worry. "How old are you, Tracker? Fifteen? Sixteen?" He lifted his head, and I winked.

"Twelve and Paxton is seven."

"You're a big kid for twelve." I didn't just say that to change the course of the conversation. The kid was tall, if a little on the thin side. His hair was straight, black, and to his shoulders. With the dark brown of his eyes, his Native American background was front and center. I glanced at his brother, and as I looked him over, I saw the resemblance between the two, but the younger one's eyes were a lighter shade of brown, and his nose was narrower with a more pointed look.

"Our mom said I get my height from my dad."

So much for lightening the conversation. And I didn't miss the fact he'd said *my* dad and not *our* dad. Which I would bet money wasn't a slip.

The receptionist called out a name, and the social worker stood. The two boys stood as well. After the woman slung her bag over her shoulder, she placed a hand on each boys' back to lead them to the front. Paxton, the youngest, stopped in front of me.

"You got kids, mister?"

I looked at him and shook my head and said, "No."

He didn't say another word. He just walked with Tracker and the social worker. I watched until the three of them disappeared through the door the receptionist was holding open for them.

"You were good with the boy." I looked at Kiyaya, who had sat quietly the whole time I talked with Tracker.

"I'm not sure what I had to say helped any. The boy's got a huge attitude."

"Unfortunately, it will not get better in foster care," Kiyaya said.

"What?" I asked as Kiyaya continued to stare at me.

"You need to find a áyat."

I ran my hand down my face. "Hell, if you're going to start that again, I just as soon you go back to being a pain in my ass and bitching about me dragging you here. It would beat hounding me about a woman."

Kiyaya smiled, and before he could respond, his name was called. He stood and so did I.

"You don't need to go back with me."

It was my turn to smile. "Oh, but I am. I want to hear from the doc's mouth, not what you tell me."

"I'm not a liar," he said, turned, and started walking.

"Didn't call you one. But intentionally omitting things will not be allowed on my watch."

"Hmm, I'm going to speak to Emilo. He needs to teach you more about respecting your elders."

"Good luck with that. You can call him later, but for now, move your ass." I followed him through the door and winked at the woman holding it open as she stared at me with wide eyes.

"Now, I know why you have no *áyat*."

I snorted as I followed him into the exam room and thought of Mac. She'd probably agree with Kiyaya.

Chapter Four

Mac

Sitting in the diner, I half listened to the conversation going on around me while I picked at my food. I'd been starved when I left the office, but now the food was unappealing to me. I didn't have to be a genius to figure out the sudden change in my appetite; it was because of the disappointing feeling I'd gotten when I walked outside, hoping to see Emery and he wasn't there. It was silly since he wasn't mentioned waiting with Devil—wishful thinking or an over exhausted mind?

We'd stood on the sidewalk while Speed and Sami shared the news of their sonogram and the picture of their son, which, of course, the men agreed with Speed on the little guy's proud pose. Ally was quiet through the exchange until Speed asked her what she thought about having a brother.

"I guess it's okay. But can I have a sister next time?"

"I'll see what I can do, baby," Speed answered, and planted a kiss on her forehead.

"Excuse me, but I'm the one who bakes it for nine months," Sami said and looked at Speed.

"And a fine job you do, babe," Speed said, then kissed Sami's forehead, too.

"Momma, can you turn up the heat next time and burn the penis off? I really want a sister."

I'd raised my hand to my mouth to muffle my laugh. Luna and Bailey didn't bother muffling theirs as we watched the men shift uncomfortably at Ally's words.

After everyone calmed down, we headed to the diner for lunch. I'd even held out hope Emery was there, only to have that illusion shattered when I walked inside, and Flirt, Carly, and Crusher were the only three seated at the table.

Didn't it figure that once I'd made my mind up not to run and face the man head-on, he was absent? My history with men was minimal because in college and medical school, I'd been too young and by the time men looked at me other than as a teenage girl, I was too focused to pay them any mind. Heck, it made me wonder if maybe he changed his mind and ran. Could I blame him if he did?

"What do you think, Mac?"

"Huh, what?" I asked as I looked up from my plate when Bailey said my name, only to find all eyes on me.

"Girl, you definitely need some sleep," Bailey said, then chuckled. "Luna asked what's the chance of telling the sex of the twins when she has her sonogram Friday?"

"Oh. Well, if they cooperate—a hundred percent."

"Awesome. They'll probably be like Speed and Sami's little dude and hide," Luna said.

"Ah, sweetheart, you already know there's two. Wouldn't you like to be surprised?" Ghost asked, then held up his hands when Luna snarled at him.

"No, I don't like surprises. Besides, we need to get their room ready, and if I know what they are, then I can decorate accordingly."

"Then I guess we'll find out Friday whether they are boys or girls," Ghost said and squeezed Luna's hand that rested on the table.

"If they're boys, can you just tell us instead of showing the picture and pointing to their junk," Flirt said while he looked at Speed, who laughed.

"You've got months. What's the hurry?" Devil asked, and I chuckled when Bailey elbowed him. "Why did you do that?"

"They are further along than I am, and I've already started on the nursery."

"No, you haven't. The room you want to use still has bedroom furniture in it," Devil said with victory in his voice that made me want to laugh because I knew Bailey had been ordering baby things.

"Lance, have you even noticed the boxes against the wall in the living room?"

"Yeah. I meant to ask you if you wanted me to haul that stuff to the Healing Hearts' place. Isn't it stuff you're getting rid of? I figured it was Neely's clothes she's grown out of weekly." Neely grinned at Devil, and he ran his hand down her face. I'd seen him do that to her a hundred times, but it still made me smile.

"How much stuff do you think Neely has, Lance? There's like ten boxes of various sizes in the room," Bailey said and shook her head when Devil shrugged.

"Brother, you got issues. I can walk in the house and know when Carly's been on a shopping spree," Crusher said and laughed when he was flipped off by Devil.

"Ah, babe, it's because I'm usually wearing what I bought, and it's more for you than me, anyway," Carly said, and Speed groaned.

"Please stop. And before you argue that you watched what you said, I'm not asking because of the little ears at the table. I'm asking as a brother who doesn't want to bleach his brain."

"No shit, we're all thankful you two started closing the bedroom window," Flirt said, then leaned up and pulled his wallet out. I watched as he pulled a dollar bill out, then he held it across the table. Ally's little hand reached out and snatched it, then she leaned back in her chair and stuffed it in the front pocket of her jeans.

I looked around the table, and everyone continued as if what happened was normal.

"Wait," I said, and all heads turned to me. "I know I'm a little tired, but why did you just pay Ally a dollar?" I looked at Flirt, but Ally answered.

"'Cause Uncle Flirt said a bad word. They all have to pay me when they say bad words." Ally blinked, and her facial expression read 'duh,' as if she'd spoken it.

"All the men in the club pay you?" I asked, and the grin that spread across Ally's face made me laugh.

When I leaned over and stuck my arm out with my hand in a fist, I knew I had moved past tired and into the space where exhaustion takes hold and the silliness surfaces. Ally bumped hers to mine, and I grinned.

"When I found out she was making them pay her, I was going to put a stop to it, but I figured the men deserved it. So, I make her put it in the bank now. By the time she's old enough for college, the cost should be covered," Sami explained.

"Roscoe's payments alone will probably cover her first year," Luna said.

"Ah, sweetheart, don't pick on Roscoe when he isn't here to defend himself," Ghost said and put his arm around Luna, then pulled her into him and kissed the top of her head. I thought what a sweet gesture, then was shocked when Luna pulled back and looked up at the man who was intimidating in size alone.

"You takin' up for Roscoe makes me wonder how much you paid shyster girl this past week." Luna narrowed her eyes at Ghost, and all he did was smile. Not saying a word. Luna then turned and looked at Ally. "Give it up, my biker babe sister."

"I made seven bucks from Uncle Ghost and eight from Uncle Dare."

Luna looked back at Ghost. "In my defense, one of the big toolboxes fell off the side of the truck and landed on mine and Dare's feet."

"Ally, what'd I tell you about tattling?" Speed asked, and I watched as Ally bit her lip as if she was thinking over his words.

"Not to do it. I didn't tattle to Momma about you paying me ten dollars when the paint can fell over and spilled on the floor," she said, then looked down at her lap.

She looked so sad; I wanted to get up and hug her.

I watched Speed look at Sami and smile, then he ran his hand over Ally's hair like he'd done to Sami in the exam room. "I'm not mad. I should have told your momma myself." When Ally looked up and met his eyes, the love reflected toward each other had a lump forming in my throat. To witness these big men melt for the women in their lives amazed me. It also had me more than a little curious if Emery would be the same way.

"I need to go to the potty, Dev," Neely said, pulling my focus away from Speed and Ally in time to watch a stricken look cross Devil's face before his eyes shot to Bailey.

"Babe?"

"She asked you. And you seriously need to get over your aversion to dealing with bodily functions."

"It isn't that. When I take her in the men's room, she asks about the urinals, and when I explained what they were for, she asked if she could pee standing up."

"Oh, for goodness sakes, take your sister to the bathroom. Go into the women's room. Thelma won't care,"

Bailey said and lifted a brow at Devil as if waiting for his next excuse.

"Fine," Devil said and glared at Bailey, who smiled back, not the least bit affected by his action. "Come on, little sis. You and me against the world," he said, grinned at Neely while he helped her out of the chair, then stuck his fist out. Neely returned his grin and bumped her little fist to his. I then watched the two hold hands and walk toward the restrooms at the back of the diner, still unsure of what I had just seen.

"Uncanny, isn't it? They look nothing alike until they smile," Carly said.

I turned and faced her. "That's it. I never noticed it before. When they do it at the same time, it's kind of creepy," I whispered the last in the hopes the others wouldn't hear, but no such luck when Carly burst out laughing.

"What's so funny?" Crusher asked Carly, who had no problem sharing what I said.

I felt my face heat with embarrassment and hoped no one would think I was making fun of Neely and Devil. I looked at Bailey apologetically, and she laughed.

"God, Mac, don't be embarrassed. We've all said the same thing. You've seen him palm her face, but you haven't seen it when Neely palms his face back, then they grin at each other. It's as if they share some weird vibe. I'd say it was because they are brother and sister, but I didn't share anything like that with James," Bailey said.

"I don't share anything with my brother either," I said.

"Well, Carly and I share nothing," Speed said as he looked in Carly's direction.

"Thank God, because you're an asshole," Carly sneered, and I giggled when Crusher snorted and Sami laughed. Carly's head whipped around to Crusher, and the look in her eyes stopped my giggles. "You can pay little miss spider monkey shyster my fee, laughing boy."

"I didn't laugh. I'm not covering your fee either, sugar. I already pay Ally enough for my own slips," Crusher said, then leaned back in his chair.

"Okay, fine. Guess when I get off shift, I'll put on my flannel PJs instead of the Victoria Secret sleepwear that came in the mail yesterday."

"Never mind, sugar, I've got your fee covered," Crusher said, already pulling his wallet out.

The only one at the table who didn't laugh was Ally. Hopefully, it was because she didn't understand what her aunt was referring to. So instead of laughing, she just stuck her hand out. Crusher dutifully set a dollar in her palm, but she didn't move her hand from the middle of the table.

"What? I didn't say one cuss word," Crusher told her.

"Aunt Carly owes me four dollars from yesterday," she replied, and I laughed so hard, I was surprised I didn't pee my pants.

Devil and Neely made it back to the table, and Bailey gave him the recap of what he'd missed. Before I knew it, I'd stopped fiddling with my food and had actually eaten it. The nourishment helped hold back the exhaustion of being sleep deprived. And in the company of friends had helped keep my thoughts from wandering too much to Emery. That part had been hard, considering everyone at the table was in a roundabout way his family. Their acceptance of me from the first time I met them was humbling.

The waitress brought the checks, and once the tabs were paid, we headed out of the diner. Everyone said goodbye and headed to their vehicles. I'd ridden with Bailey and Devil, and as I started to get in, Flirt pulled the door open for me. He'd parked his bike behind Devil's truck.

"He went to the reservation to visit his gramps. Well, technically, his great gramps. Kiyaya's sick, and he went to check on him."

"Okay."

Flirt's lips twitched. "Just thought you might want to know why you haven't seen him around."

I got into the vehicle and looked back at Flirt. "It isn't any of my business where Emery goes."

Flirt snorted, then smirked. "I'll let you continue to pretend you weren't looking for him. But, Doc, I can guarantee when he gets back in town, he'll be looking for you." He closed the door and walked back to his bike.

I glanced to the front at Devil and Bailey. "That almost sounded like a threat. What did he mean, Emery will look for me?"

Devil laughed, and Bailey smacked his shoulder. "Oh, he's probably talked to Coast, that's all, and was just letting you know where he is. Umm… Coast looking for you… I'm not sure what he meant by that."

Devil snorted as he pulled out of the parking spot, and Bailey glared at him. I looked over at Neely, who was in her car seat, and she shrugged and smiled at me. I felt at that moment everyone was privy to something I had no clue about. Even a four-year-old little girl.

Devil dropped Bailey and me off in front of the office, then drove away.

"Four more hours and we're done for the day. For your sake, I hope no one goes into labor tonight and get some sleep," Bailey said as I tried the door and it opened, which meant Amelia had beaten us back from lunch.

"You and me both. I plan to go home, soak in the bathtub, then fall into bed until the alarm clock wakes me in the morning," I said as we reached the receptionist area that already had a few patients waiting in it.

"Right on time, ladies," Amelia said and handed charts over the counter to Bailey.

"I'll get the rooms set up," she said as she flipped through the charters.

"Sounds good. I'll be ready in five. Let me hang my jacket and hit the restroom, and then we'll get these next four hours knocked out," I said and headed to my office.

The hours flew by and with no 'in labor' interruptions. I even got to enjoy the bubble bath when I got home. The solid night's sleep was a different matter.

At four in the morning, the phone rang. It seemed another one of my patient's baby didn't get the memo that I needed sleep. I was up, dressed, and on my way to the hospital in under twenty.

Babies waited for no one.

Chapter Five

Coast

"I'm going to go to the store today. Anything you need?" I asked as I washed the skillet.

It had been four days since I'd taken Kiyaya to the clinic, and the improvement was noticeable, but it would be weeks before the bronchitis cleared. It also had been four days of constant arguments about getting the man to take the antibiotics and using the inhaler that was prescribed. The doctor informed Kiyaya that if he hadn't come into the clinic, he would have more than likely been in the hospital by month's end with pneumonia. The bacterial infection was contained to the bronchial tubes but could have easily moved into his lungs, which would have hampered his breathing even more.

"Licorice, the red kind," he answered from the table where he sat finishing the omelet and toast I'd made.

"Didn't we buy like two packages of that stuff at the drugstore?" My nose crinkled with the thought of how nasty that stuff was.

"It's black licorice. I like the red, too."

It didn't escape me that my great grandfather was more than surly. I'd chalked it up to not feeling well, but he was on the mend. Not that the man hadn't acted like a five-year-old over taking his medicine, it was that his attitude had gotten worse when I mentioned last night I was planning to head home in the next day or so.

"If you want to go with me to the store, you'll need to bundle up. It's windy as hell outside." I walked to the table, sat, and picked up my coffee.

"I don't need you to tell me about the weather. I don't need you to go to the store for me. Or chop wood or work on my truck. You can go home today," Kiyaya said, then pushed his chair back and grabbed his empty plate and silverware off the table.

I didn't respond right away to his outburst. I leisurely took a drink of coffee and watched as he stood at the sink, washing his dishes.

"You already tired of me being around, *xwísaat*?"

"Old man, my ass. You treat me like a *miyánash*."

I snorted, and he turned and glared at me. "Maybe because you have been acting like a child," I said and cocked an eyebrow and stared back at him.

"It has been good having you here," he answered, and seemed embarrassed about admitting it.

I let the fact he put up no argument about acting like a child go and replied, "I've enjoyed being here." And I honestly had. I'd already planned to visit him more often, and maybe if I pushed enough, I'd get him off the reservation to visit me.

"Maybe tonight I'll let you win at checkers," he said and smiled.

I laughed, stood, then carried my coffee cup to the sink. I placed a hand on his shoulder and gave a small squeeze, then said, "Who says I haven't been letting you win?"

"Ha! You have always been a terrible player." He chuckled and patted my hand that still rested on his shoulder.

"And I see you still like to gloat. You even did it when I was just a kid, too. So much for being an elder and helping to frame young minds. You could have let me win one game."

"What would that have taught you?"

"That my great grandfather cared enough to throw a game for me."

"I cared enough *not* to throw a game for you. Life is hard. It's harder when prejudices exist. You don't sit around and wait for someone to give you something, or you'll have nothing. If you work and get things on your own, they have more value to you."

"I'm talking about one game of checkers. One hand of cards. Not prejudices and life. Christ knows I've dealt with enough of them—it only fueled me to work harder."

"And you felt better because you achieved the things on your own, Emery."

I blew out a breath. "Tell me we did not have this…" I waved my hand around life altering conversation… because I did shit around here for you. Seriously?" I ran my hand down my face, then looked back at Kiyaya. His expression told me I was right.

"I enjoy doing for myself. Just as you do."

"You might as well get over it. I'll be back in a few weeks with a couple of my brothers to fix the roof and replace the damn windows."

"I don't need you to fix those things for me."

"Goddammit, you got no business on a roof, and you sure as shit can't yank those old ass windows out by yourself. Sue me for loving you enough to not want it to rain on your head inside your house. Or for you to freeze to death because the windows can't keep the cold from entering."

Kiyaya stared at me and said, "*Átawit* you, Emery." Then he started walking away. "Let me get my coat, and I'll ride to the store with you. If I don't, you will buy the wrong stuff."

"Love you, you crusty old Indian," I said to his back as he headed into his bedroom.

"Pain in the ass half breed," he yelled over his shoulder.

I snorted. "You know that shit isn't politically correct, right? If anyone else called me that, I'd kick their ass," I said and grabbed my jacket off the back of the chair and pulled it on.

"Eh, I'm too old to care what others think. And like with the checkers, you'll not win against me," he answered as he walked back into the room with his coat on.

Shaking my head and chuckling, I went to the door and opened it. "Come on. Let's get the shopping done and get back so we can play more checkers. I'm feeling lucky today."

"Eh, you gonna need more than luck," Kiyaya said as he passed by me and headed for his truck.

I got in the driver's side and started the truck, then pulled out onto the road. I glanced over at Kiyaya. He was looking out the window. I focused back on the road and thought about how disappointed I was when I received Suni's call. It came at an inconvenient time because I was ready to make my move with Mac. But after spending time with Kiyaya, minus the arguments, I was glad I'd made the trip. There'd be plenty of time to spend with Mac, which I planned on doing as soon as I pulled back into town tomorrow. She and I had danced around each other long enough.

"I don't need all that food," Kiyaya said as I placed the bags in the back of the pickup.

"Four bags of groceries doesn't amount to a lot of food. It's mostly cans of soup and simple things for you to heat while you are recuperating. You're just mad I refused to let you pay."

"I have money."

I counted to ten in my head because I knew it was hard for him to accept help. But for fuck's sake, we're family. "I know. I also know you are on a fixed income. So, this month you have a little extra left to splurge with."

"I don't want you wasting your money on me. You need to save so you can support a family one day."

"If I couldn't afford to do it, I wouldn't. I've got enough money. Besides, maybe I'll find me a sugar momma." I grinned, thinking about what Mackenzie would say if she heard me say that.

"Hmm… you better start looking. You're not getting any younger, *áswan*."

"It has been a long time since I was a boy. And I might surprise you and bring a woman with me when I come back," I said jokingly, but the thought stuck. I wondered what it would take to get Mac to come with me and what she would think if she did?

"You know our people haven't stolen women for over a hundred and seventy-five years," Kiyaya replied, then chuckled as he opened the passenger side door.

"I'm hurt you think I'd have to steal a woman. For all you know, I could have ten hidden away," I said after I opened the other door.

"Why are they hidden? Are they ugly?"

"I can't win with you. Get in the truck and let's go home," I said as I prepared to get into the vehicle. I stopped when I noticed the woman approaching from the sidewalk in front of us. "Ma'am!" She turned when I yelled.

"Yes." She stopped walking.

"You're the social worker who was at the clinic with the two boys?" I asked.

I saw the recognition on her face even before she answered, "Yes, I'm a caseworker with the ICWA, Indian Child Welfare Act. You sat beside us. What can I do for you?"

"How's Tracker and Paxton adjusting?"

Her eyebrows scrunched together, and by her expression, I was expecting to get the spill on not being allowed to talk about them. I totally understood privacy acts, but I didn't want all the details about their case, which I didn't need considering it wasn't hard to figure out the circumstances that had the two boys going into the system after conversing with Tracker. I just wanted to know if the two of them were doing okay.

I was shocked when she looked around, then stepped off the sidewalk and moved closer.

"I shouldn't be saying anything to you, but you helped. After talking with you, Tracker started cooperating instead of fighting me every step."

"So, he and Paxton are doing okay?"

"We're waiting for a foster family with room to take on two. Temporarily, we've had to split the boys between two fosters until one becomes available. Neither boy is happy, but Paxton is doing somewhat better with the arrangement than Tracker."

"Two more kids who get lost in the system. What bullshit."

"They're not lost, Mister?"

"Cortez."

"Like I was saying, they aren't lost, Mr. Cortez. We do the best we can to keep siblings together. The system isn't without flaws, and sometimes circumstances place us in a bind. As soon as a foster family becomes available, Tracker and Paxton will be placed in the new home together."

"So, in the meantime, two boys, brothers no less, who have relied on each other for their entire lives, are the ones expected to adjust and deal with another shitty situation thrown at them by adults. Adults responsible for their care and to protect them. Seems nobody has ever protected them."

"Mr. Cortez, we placed the boys with wonderful foster parents. They will be watched after and taken care of. I promise."

"Miss, Mrs.?"

"Mrs. Stone. Cassandra Stone."

"Mrs. Stone, I'm not laying fault on you. When I said lost in the system, I didn't mean physically. I meant mentally. At least in Tracker and Paxton's case. I'm not naïve to think their circumstance is the first your agency has dealt with. But they are the first I've interacted with personally. If only for a few minutes. I'm astute, Mrs. Stone. I was trained to be by the military. I don't have to read the file on Tracker and Paxton to know they are or were kids of a drug addict. They said as much. There probably isn't any father listed on either birth certificate because she never knew who the fathers were. She kept the kids because she figured she could get more government assistance. More funds for her habit. She

74

wasn't interested in whether they ate, were clean, nothing to do with them mattered. So, two boys banded together to watch after each other. The majority left for Tracker because he's the oldest. Hell, they probably had to take care of their mother when she binged. Now they are two mixed-race kids, expected to accept their fate when they don't feel they fit in anywhere. We both know even here on the reservation there are prejudices. And now, they don't even have each other to lean on. I saw the defeat in Tracker's eyes the other day. The longer he is separated from Paxton, the worse he will act out. You and I both know what happens then. They will rotate him in and out of a dozen or more foster homes until he hits eighteen and kicked to the curb."

"Were you a product of the foster care system, Mr. Cortez?"

"No, but I could have been if it wasn't for my great grandfather…" I pointed to Kiyaya, who was in the car listening to mine and Mrs. Stone's conversation. "and a dad who fought to keep me. Society isn't kind when you are in the minority. Sometimes it isn't kind even when you are the majority. I'll admit there were times I struggled to balance the two sides of me, but I had support and people around me who didn't care about my mother being a doper, or care that my skin was darker—they taught me it wasn't a flaw in me, but in the other person if they couldn't get past my ethnicity. I've dealt with what Tracker and Paxon will have to face, whether in foster care or after they age out. So please make sure they get reunited soon. They are going to need each other."

"I'll do everything in my power to make that happen, Mr. Cortez."

"Great. And sorry for the rant. I guess the boys left an impression on me."

Mrs. Stone smiled. "It happens. Have you ever considered applying to be a foster parent, Mr. Cortez?"

I snorted and looked down at the cut I wore, then back to Mrs. Stone. "I don't think the state of Washington would approve of turning kids over to a biker. A single one at that."

"You never know until you apply." She glanced at Kiyaya, then back at me. "It was good chatting with you, Mr. Cortez."

"You, too. And again, sorry for going off on a rant."

"It shows you care, Mr. Cortez. Caring makes for a good foster." Mrs. Stone turned and walked toward the entrance of the store.

When I got in the truck and closed the door, Kiyaya spoke, "She's right."

I started the truck and backed out of the spot. "About what?"

"You do care."

"That may be, but I think it takes more than caring to be a good foster."

"Maybe. But caring is the first step," Kiyaya said, then turned and started looking out the side window.

The drive back to Kiyaya's was quiet, and I thought of Tracker and Paxton. I hoped Mrs. Stone kept her word about getting the two reunited quickly. Crusher, Speed,

Devil, Flirt, and Jag weren't brothers by blood, they were much better. I couldn't imagine after growing up together, what it would have been like to be suddenly separated. It'd been hard enough when we went our separate ways at eighteen.

I had decided by the time we got to the house that I would check in with Mrs. Stone about the boys when I came back in a few weeks.

Once we were back home, the rest of the day was relaxing, and Kiyaya and I spent the evening playing checkers.

I didn't win a single game.

Friday morning rolled around, and after breakfast and making sure Kiyaya understood when to take his antibiotics, I packed my things in my saddlebags.

"I'll call and let you know when I'll be back. It shouldn't take too long to get the windows in. You have enough wood chopped and groceries for at least a week or two. And don't throw the medicine in the trash after I leave."

"You worry like a *lmamá*," Kiyaya griped from the couch.

"If the old woman's shoe fits. I don't want to haul your old ass back to the clinic again."

"I will take the medicine, Emery."

"Alright. Well, I'm going to hit the road," I said. "Love ya, *xwísaat* (old man)."

Kiyaya stood and walked to the door where I stood with my bags. "*Átawit* you, *áswan* (love you, boy)."

I dropped my bags and hugged the stubborn old man. "No wild parties while I'm gone."

"Eh."

After I released him, I picked up my saddlebags and went out the door. Once I'd fastened them, I mounted my bike. I looked over my shoulder before I turned onto the main road and saw Kiyaya in the doorway watching, and I threw my hand up. When my bike hit the blacktop, I cut loose on the throttle and headed home.

On the ride, I had plenty of time to think of Mac. I hoped she was ready because I had miles of riding to plan my attack.

Chapter Six

Mac

"Two boys," Luna said on repeat as we stood at the receptionist's desk to schedule her next appointment.

"I explained mono-amniotic twins to you," I said and chuckled when Luna rolled her eyes.

"Yeah, yeah. They share everything, except they each have their own cord. I'll tell you what they share—my sanity. I'm as big as Sami, and her due date is before mine. They could have been girls and saved me at least some stretch marks. But no, two boys that are the size of this one." She pointed to Ghost, who stood beside her, still holding and staring at the sonogram snapshot of his sons.

"They won't come out his size. You know that, right?" Bailey said and earned a glare from Luna.

"Duh. But considering the space they go through to get out, they might as well be Brax's size."

I patted Luna's shoulder. "You got this. Everything is progressing normally, and you are gaining weight accordingly for someone carrying twins. Besides, the epidural will help with the pain during delivery, and I imagine you will be like the other mothers when it is over, and you are holding them in your arms—everything you went through prior will be forgotten. If it didn't work that way, most women would never have another child."

"Ha! I can tell you right now, I'm not going through this again," Luna sneered, and when Ghost bent and kissed the top of her head, she looked up at him. "Don't think I don't know what you are doing? Placating me."

"I wouldn't dream of doing that, sweetheart. Especially when you are giving me such a gift. Not one child, but two. I love you, baby."

"Ahh, I love you, too," Luna said and leaned her forehead against his chest. Ghost kissed the top of her head again, then looked over at Bailey and me with a huge smile. Then he winked.

I shook my head and grinned back. After witnessing the interactions between the men and their women since getting to know them, the men made it pretty hard for their women to refuse them anything. Case in point, the only one not pregnant out of the women was Carly, and per her, it wasn't from lack of trying.

"Well, I need to get back to work," I abruptly said and walked away, not waiting for any replies. I didn't even have to look over my shoulder to know my brisk departure had left them curious.

I walked into my office and closed the door, leaning against it, then swiped at my eyes. Periods of time passed, and not once would I think of the reason for switching my fields of study. Then suddenly, the smallest of things would bring tears to my eyes, reminding me I'd never know the joy of bringing a life into the world of my own. I shared in others' happiness.

There were times I'd tell myself it didn't matter, and I could have a well-rounded life with a good man and be happy. Other times, it felt out of reach. Emery pursued me now, but if he wanted a family like his friends and brothers, would he change his mind about me?

I walked to my desk, grabbed a tissue, and wiped my face. I needed to put the negative thoughts back in their box and continue my day. There were expectant mothers counting on me.

As Bailey and I walked out of the exam room, Amelia was headed in our direction.

"Doctor Minton, the hospital called. Kate Winston arrived by ambulance. She's in labor and bleeding."

"Oh, no. Bailey…" I started.

"I got it. Go, I'll take care of what I can, and Amelia can reschedule the rest."

"Thanks," I said, already halfway to my office.

After arriving at the hospital and entering the ER, I checked with the desk to see if Kate was there or if they moved her to labor and delivery. As I rode the elevator up, I said a small prayer for Kate and Larry Winston and their unborn daughter.

Kate Winston was a thirty-six-year-old first-time mother-to-be diagnosed with preeclampsia at twenty-one weeks. She also suffered from hypertension. It had been a battle keeping her blood pressure down throughout her pregnancy.

I pushed through the door of the room Kate was in. Mr. Winston stood on the side of the bed, holding his wife's hand as he tried to stay out of the way while Kate was being taken care of. She already was hooked up to the machine to keep track of her vitals, and the nurse was presently attaching the monitor to her stomach for the baby.

"How are you doing, Kate?" I asked as I picked up the chart and read what they had noted before I arrived.

"Been better. I'm worried, Dr. Minton. It's too early for her," Kate said, and her voice cracked at the end.

"You're at twenty-eight and a half weeks. Is it ideal? No. But it's doable. So let's not worry yet, okay? Your blood pressure is high enough right now. Can you tell me what you experienced today, yesterday? Cramps, discomfort?" I asked as I moved to the bottom of the bed.

"Yesterday was fine. This morning I woke up, and while Larry was getting ready for work, I went to the kitchen to fix him a cup of coffee and breakfast. I had a little discomfort in my back, but I figured I'd laid wrong or something. After Larry left for work, I straightened the kitchen, then went to take a shower, thinking the warm water would help my back. As I washed, that's when I noticed the blood."

While she talked, I pulled on gloves and checked her. She was bleeding, and though it looked like a lot right now, it was mild.

"Right now, it's mild. We'll monitor it to make sure that doesn't change. The baby is okay for now, too, which is what we want. I'm more worried about you. We need to get your blood pressure down because that isn't good for you. We don't want it to spike, it could put you both at risk."

"Is that what's causing her to bleed, Doc?" Larry asked.

"To an extent. But it isn't solely responsible. The bleeding is more than likely from a placenta abruption. It means the placenta is pulling away from the uterine wall too early. Kate's problem is the hypertension diagnosis before the pregnancy, it escalated. Preeclampsia is from normal level HBP turning chronic because of the pregnancy. Placenta abruptions are a part of it all." I walked over and looked at the readout on the EFM (electronic fetal monitor). The fetal heartbeat was good, and so were the oxygen levels, but Kate was also having mild uterine contractions.

When I looked back at her, I watched her twinge, then she reached and rubbed above where the monitor was strapped.

"When did the twinging start?"

"It was right before Larry got home. I called him after I got out of the shower after seeing the blood."

"I called an ambulance after I arrived home. I was afraid to drive and have something happen with her while we were in the car," Larry replied.

"You did the right thing. No reason to take unnecessary chances. I'm going to have the nurse administer some meds for your blood pressure."

"Will that stop the labor?" Larry asked.

"It's a possibility, but the high blood pressure is just one factor, Mr. Winston. The placenta abruption is the major issue. The fetus gets its oxygen that way. I discussed with you both about the probability of this happening. Labor would be induced or even a caesarian because it won't just be the baby at risk."

"What's the likelihood of putting off delivery longer? Giving the baby a better chance," Kate asked.

I laid my hand on top of hers, then gave it a reassuring squeeze. "We can't. The risk to you and the baby won't allow it."

"If the baby is born today, what are we facing medically with her, Doc?"

I saw the worry in Mr. Winston's eyes for his child and wife. I would have given anything to take it away, but that was beyond my power. Life's fragile even under perfect circumstances.

"She'll weigh anywhere from two and a quarter to two and a half pounds. Once delivered, we'll do nasal intubation to help her breathe until her lungs develop. Babies born this early, besides the low weight, almost always have breathing issues. She'll be moved to NICU. The placenta coming detached early not only affects the oxygen but blood flow, too. That can cause other issues. Let's worry about issues after the birth and concentrate on lowering Kate's HBP. The lower we get it before delivery, the less strain on mother and daughter."

"How long will the baby have to stay in NICU?" Kate asked, and continued to rub her hand over her belly.

"It can depend on what complications arise. One step at a time, Kate. Let's get her here first. Okay?"

"Okay. We plan to use Dr. Agassi as the baby's pediatrician," Kate said, and looked at her husband.

"A few friends of mine take their children to Dr. Agassi. They like her. Her office is in the building beside mine, but I've only talked with her twice in passing since she opened her practice. You'll have paperwork to fill out, and if you put her name down as the baby's pediatrician, the neonatal staff will make sure she's aware of everything, so when the baby's released from NICU, she will do all follow-ups from then on."

"Thank you, Dr. Minton," Mr. Winston said, and I smiled.

"You're welcome. I'm going to step out and check in with my office and make arrangements in case a c-section is required. I'll be down the hall if you need me. Try to relax, okay?" The parents nodded, and I left the room.

Far from out of the woods with the baby, I would do my best to bring her into the world. Once she was born, hopefully, her stay in the NICU would be short, but first, I had to give her a fighting chance. At almost twenty-nine weeks, the odds were on her side.

Two hours later, Styrofoam cup of coffee in hand, on my way to check in on Kate Winston, I met the nurse coming out of her room.

"Oh good, I was coming to get you. The bleeding has picked up."

"How's her HBP?"

"It has lowered, but not by much."

"Alright, make sure an OR is available. Call the NICU and tell them we are going to need them."

"You got it."

I went into the room, and after checking Kate, I read the monitor tape. The oxygen level and blood flow to the baby were dropping.

"Well, are you ready to become parents?" I asked as cheerfully as I could. I learned the more relaxed I was, the parents stayed calmer.

"Do we have a choice?" Kate asked and gave a weak smile.

"I wish I could give one," I said as the door opened and a nurse walked in with an orderly following behind her.

"Everything is ready. Neonatal is on their way," the nurse said, and then we went into action.

Chapter Seven

Coast

I turned on the street where Mac's clinic was and smiled when I noticed Devil sitting in his truck out front of the building. He glanced up in the mirror as I pulled in behind him.

I took off my helmet and dismounted as he exited the truck and walked toward me with his hand stuck out. I grasped his hand, then pulled him in for a man hug.

"You just get back into town?"

"Nah, I got in a few hours ago. I stopped by my place first and dumped my stuff. Swung by my dad's place, but he wasn't home, so I'll catch up with him tomorrow. Then I stopped by the shop to check in with you guys. Instead, I walked in with Jag dealing with Poppy. Guess he, Crusher, Speed, and Flirt were going over a design, and he turned around to check on her when she'd gone quiet. She'd somehow gotten her pants down and pulled her diaper off. A poop filled one, and she'd smeared it on herself and all over the playpen before he caught her."

"Damn, now I'm glad I wasn't there. I can't deal with that stuff."

"Well, you better start finding a way. You got less than what? Seven months."

"Yeah, yeah, that's what Bailey says." Devil snorted. "Did Speed whip out the picture to show you?"

I chuckled. "Yes, he did. He said Sami threatened to tear it up if he didn't stop showing it to everyone."

"He's shown it to most of the club. Did you hear Ghost and Luna's are having twin boys? Going to have three boys and three girls running around here."

"Numbers could shift depending what Bailey and River have." I cocked a brow at Devil.

"Shit, I didn't think of that. Well, if the numbers stay even. I hope Bay and I have the boy. River and Jag can have the girl. After today, I'm not sure I can handle another girl."

I frowned. "Did something happen today? No one mentioned it while I was at the shop."

"Yeah, it was why I wasn't there. I was at the elementary school. Neely got in trouble. She's at Sue's place with Sami and Ally. She's been in school three whole days. Ally got in trouble, too. Along with Dr. Agassi's little girl, Sawyer."

"Why does Dr. Agassi sound familiar?" I asked.

"She's Ally and Neely's pediatrician. Her practice is right there." Devil pointed to the building beside Mac's.

"Okay, I don't know Sawyer, but I can see Ally in trouble. Neely's always sweet and shy, though. What the hell did she get in trouble for?"

"Brother, little girls are vicious, I tell ya. I learned that today. My sister, who comes across as shy and quiet most of the time, punched a first grader in the stomach, then when the kid bent over, she belted him in the nose."

I stared at Devil, then burst out laughing. "Neely, who is in preschool, not only kicked a first grader's ass, but a boy?" I laughed harder.

"Oh, save your laughter 'cause the shit gets worse. Let me tell you the complete story. Which I had to listen to from the principal. First, picture Sami sitting on one side of me, and Brie, that's Dr. Agassi's first name, sitting on my other side. All three of us are in chairs in front of the principal's desk. Neely, Ally, and Sawyer were sitting on a couch against the wall. Unaffected by being in the principal's office because they were in trouble. Which makes me wonder exactly how often the girls have been in the principal's office. It brought back too many memories for me, and I thought I was going to break out in hives.

"Anyway, the kids had been outside on the playground since it was nice out. The kids in preschool, kindergarten, and first grade share playground time. Well, Anthony, the first-grade boy, swiped a Pokémon, Star Wars, or some damn card of Benji's when he set it down on the bench to take off his hat and put it in his jacket pocket. Benji asked the kid to give it back, and the kid shoved him down and told Benji he didn't take his card.

"Ally, of course, gets involved, since she considers Benji her friend now. I'm never gonna understand girls' minds work, brother. Never. Anyway, Anthony then shoves Ally, which brings her new friend Sawyer, into the picture. Sawyer interrogates Anthony. Asking him questions, like: why was he standing so close to the bench? Wasn't he supposed to be on his side of the playground with the other first-graders? Did he see the card and decide to take it?"

"Hold up. Sawyer is in kindergarten?" I interrupted Devil and asked.

"Yeah. Brie admitted to the principal that maybe she shouldn't watch law enforcement shows while Sawyer is around, and the principal agreed. Anthony didn't like getting questioned, so he told Sawyer to shut up and called her a stupid girl. That's when Neely got into the mix. She was supposed to be with her class, but had walked over where Ally was. She told Anthony he was the stupid one, then punched him twice. Ally takes the card out of Anthony's coat pocket while he is holding his face where Neely punched him. Ally gives the card back to Benji and tells Anthony people who steal always are caught because karma is a bitch."

"Christ, that sounds like something Carly would say," I said.

"Yes, Sami said that, too. Bailey's going to band the watching of UFC fights once I tell her what happened."

"Come on, admit it. The shit is funny."

"Hell, brother, my sister is a closet badass." Devil chuckled, and we bumped fists.

"The way she strikes, we should call her cobra," I said as Bailey walked out of the clinic.

"Call who cobra?" she asked as she turned and locked the door.

I ignored Bailey's question and instead asked one of my own, "Did Mac go out the back?"

"No, she's at the hospital."

Devil snickered, and I glanced over at him. "Well, well. It's about time, brother. Flirt was right."

"Flirt?"

"Yeah, we had lunch at the diner Monday, and Mac joined us. Flirt told her you were out of town, and she tried to play it off as if she wasn't concerned. Act as if she didn't understand why Flirt was telling her. He went along with her charade, then told her she'd know soon enough why you being out of town would be her business."

"Terrific," I said and shook my head. "Guess I'll catch you guys later." I turned toward my bike.

"Tell Mac we said hi," Devil commented, and Bailey giggled.

Mac had already been a skittish around me, and if Flirt made it worse, I was going to kick his ass. I got on my bike and took off in the hospital's direction.

As I entered the hospital, I headed for the reception desk. The woman behind the counter verified Mac was still on the maternity floor after I had flirted relentlessly and told her I'd wanted to surprise my woman since I gotten back in town early than she was expecting me. I went and sat down to wait. Mac would have to pass me on her way out.

Chapter Eight

Mac

The surgery took twenty minutes from start to finish. Both the mom and baby had come through with flying colors. Bethany Nicole Winston weighed two and a quarter pounds and measured fourteen and a half inches. She'd given me a small whimper after pulling her out. It was the best sound in the world.

Now Bethany's new life care would be up to the neonatal unit. Afterwards, I'd stayed and monitored Kate to make sure she suffered no complications. Her blood pressure dropped into a good range not too long after delivery. It was a good sign. When Kate was ready, they would take her and Larry to NICU to spend time with their daughter.

Three hours later, after delivering the preemie, I stood in the hallway watching the new parents through the glass.

I watched Larry as he placed a hand on Kate's shoulder and bent and kissed the top of her head. He whispered something in her ear, and a smile spread across her face.

If I ever doubted changing specialties, it only took seeing the happiness of a new family to know it had been the right decision.

"Heading out, Dr. Minton?" the neonatal resident asked as he approached, pulling me away from my musing.

"Yes, I just wanted to have a peek before I left. How's the Winston baby doing?" I asked, then rubbed my hand across the back of my neck.

"Other than her lung development and weight, she is doing remarkably well. You've had a long afternoon?"

"I've had a long week."

"I hear ya. Have a good evening, and hopefully, no more of your patients decide to go into labor today."

"Bite your tongue. Don't jinks me." After a few more words with the resident, I headed toward the elevators.

Inside the elevator, I leaned against the wall and pulled out my phone. With it being six-thirty, the office would be closed, meaning I didn't feel obligated to swing by before I headed home. I had no messages from Bailey, and when I'd talked with her earlier, she'd had everything under control.

The elevator dinged, and I pushed away from the wall as the door slid open. God, I was tired, but the week had ended on a pleasant note, and I couldn't complain about that. Not when it could have ended tragically.

Thinking of the tiny baby girl with the barely developed dark eyelashes, I smiled. Would there ever come a time that bringing life into the world got to be routine? I surely hoped it didn't.

With my head bent, scrolling my phone, I walked across the lobby toward the hospital's exit doors. When I bumped into a hard body, I automatically responded, "Oh, sorry."

"You look dead on your feet, Doc."

I jerked my head up. "What are you doing here?"

Coast

After an hour or so of waiting, I watched Mac step off the elevator. I stood and moved into her path and stopped. She wasn't even paying attention as she walked, looking down at her phone. I briefly wondered how many times she'd made the same trip through the hospital, since she didn't need to look up to see where she was going.

She looked beat, and I might have worried something had gone wrong if not for the slight smile on her face.

Compared to me, she was so small. She moved closer and closer, and when she had almost reached me, I stepped directly in front of her, leaving her no room other than to bump into me.

"Oh, sorry."

"You look dead on your feet, Doc." Her head jerked up at my words.

"What are you doing here?"

"Looking for you. I went by your office first, and Bailey told me you were here."

"Oh. So why did you come by the office?"

I stared at her for a moment before responding, "Because we have unfinished business."

"It's going to have to wait. I'm exhausted. I'm going home and getting some sleep," she said and tried to step around me, but I moved with her.

"I'll take you home. You shouldn't be driving. Come on." I knew I was being pushy, but the woman was looking as if she would drop at any minute. I shifted and placed a hand on her back and started leading her out of the hospital.

"I'm capable of driving myself home."

"It will not hurt to leave your car here. I'll bring you by tomorrow to get it," I said as we walked outside. When she shivered, I sighed and questioned, "You didn't wear a jacket or coat to the hospital?"

"It's in my car."

"Well, we're going to have to get it. Otherwise, you'll freeze to death on the back of my bike. Where are you parked?" I looked around the lot for her small SUV.

"Over there." She pointed to a row of vehicles off to the side, and I led us in that direction.

When we reached her vehicle, she pulled the keys out of her pocket and used the fob to unlock the doors. She opened the door behind the driver's seat and pulled out her jacket. I helped her put it on and then turned her around to face me and fastened it.

"I can handle zipping my coat," she said as she looked up at me. "And since I'm at my car, I'll drive home. There is no sense in you taking me home and then having to come back to town tomorrow just to pick me up, to take me to pick my car up."

"Come on, Doc. Don't fight me. Let me take you home and feed you. You'll feel better."

I thought she was going to fight me. Instead, she conceded with, "Okay."

After making sure her car was locked, I led her across the lot to my bike. She stood beside it as I pulled out the extra helmet I'd stashed early and handed it to her.

"I'm not sure what's at my house to fix," she said as she put the helmet on, and I helped her fasten it.

I waited to answer until we were on my bike, ready to pull out. "Then it's a good thing we are going to my house," I said, then started slowly to the exit.

"You purposely waited to tell me we were going to your house," she yelled into my ear as she held onto me.

"At my house, I've got steaks, potatoes to bake, and the fixings to load on them."

"You had this planned."

"The cool, fresh air must be kicking your brain in. You're catching on." I barely felt the smack on my back. "You better hang on, Doc. I'd hate for you to slide off the back."

"You're an arrogant ass," she yelled.

"So you've told me," I snorted and kicked the bike speed up a notch once I felt her arms tighten around me.

When she snuggled closer and laid her head on my back, it was the best feeling. At least now. Hopefully, after a little nourishment and rest, I'd have her legs wrapped around me and I imagined no other feeling could top that.

Chapter Nine

Mac

I snuggled closer and laid my head against Emery's back to absorb the warmth that flowed from him. The air had turned colder as the sun went down, which made the ride toward his home at the Black Hawk compound more than a little chilly, making me thankful for the large body blocking most of the wind in front of me.

When I bumped into Emery at the hospital, literally, I'd been surprised at first, but then worry struck me he might be hurt and was waiting to be seen. I'd discreetly checked him over to make sure.

In true form, though, he'd taken control of the moment and led me out of the hospital. My mind still reeled from the Winston delivery and their tiny little girl in NICU. But by the time I realized what the man was doing, I was behind him on his bike.

As my head cleared from the brisk air outside, I knew he purposely left out that he was taking me to his home, not mine.

Heat touched my calf, and I opened my eyes. I hadn't even realized I closed them. I glanced down and saw Emery's gloved hand on my lower leg. He rubbed his hand up and down, then gave my calf a squeeze before he moved his hand back to the handlebar on his bike. The heat of his touch along with it.

As the miles ate away, my stomach tightened. I'd run from the man every time I saw him for the better part of a year. Dodged him because deep down, from the minute he sat in the chair beside me in the diner, I'd known. I'd known if I allowed him to get close to me, it would be easy to lean on him. I smiled at how ironic it was that I was now doing that very thing.

I'd called him arrogant at every opportunity. Part to get under his skin with the hope he'd walk away. Also, to remind me he wasn't for me. I'd moved to Shades Valley because it'd been a place I'd enjoyed as a child when I'd visited my grandparents with my parents and brother. A place of comfort when I'd needed it most. I'd left Maryland without a backward glance, drove across the country, rented a condominium, then invested the inheritance from my parents and bought an already established practice from its 'looking to retire' doctor. None of my planning had included the man in front of me.

The bike slowed, then turned left. I lifted my head and grasped tighter onto Emery. When we reached the gate that stood open, he slowed as we rode through, giving a wave to the young biker who'd walked out of the small building that sat to one side. We'd passed the clubhouse, then headed down the road where six nicely built log homes sat.

I knew they were each similar on the inside, though I'd only been in three of them; Sami and Speed's, Carly and Crusher's, and Bailey and Devil's.

As we rode past, I noticed lights on in each of the homes, signifying the others were home. Emery drove around the back of his home, where a two-bay detached garage was. He stopped in front of it.

"Jump off, *cariño*," he said. I had to hold on to his shoulder and slide to the side until my foot touched the ground, which allowed me to swing my other leg over. As I worked to get myself off the bike, one door on the garage opened.

When I stood on the ground, Emery chuckled and shook his head, then turned the bike and backed it into the garage. I held the helmet out to him after he had got off the bike. After he put away the helmets, we walked out, and the door closed behind us.

"Yo!"

I jumped at the voice, and Emery put his arm around my shoulder and pulled me in to his side.

"Sorry, Mackenzie. I didn't mean to scare you," Flirt said as he cut across the yard and into view.

"It's okay. I didn't see you. It's pretty dark out here, even with the house lights on. Plus, I've noticed none of you make noise when you walk," I said as he approached.

"Why are you out wandering around?" Emery asked him.

"Power blinked a bit ago. Thought I better check on the generator. Filled it up in case the power goes out for real. When I saw you pull in, I wanted to let you know about the power and that I checked on your generator, too. Didn't know how late you would be out?"

"Appreciate it, brother."

"Do you lose power out this way often?" I asked as I looked around. I could see lights through the windows of the homes. And several strategically placed outdoor lights mounted. I noticed them the first time I'd come to the compound to visit Bailey, but I had paid little attention when I left.

"Not too often, but when it goes out, sometimes they take a while to get around to us, since we're outside of town. A generator pumps enough power to keep the fridge running and a light or two on," Emery answered.

"I bet it's spooky out here when there're no lights at all." There might be houses and the large clubhouse on the compound, but most of the land surrounding the area was woods.

"It can be," Emery said, then I felt the vibrations of Emery's body as he chuckled. "The club hasn't always had the generators, though. Our dads talked about getting them, but they kept putting off purchasing them since we don't lose power that often. Devil was the reason they finally equipped each house and the clubhouse with them."

"Shit, what were we? Seven or eight." Flirt grinned. "Damn, if I close my eyes and think about it, I can still feel the burn on my ass from the spanking my dad gave me."

"Hell, brother, I not only got a spanking from my dad. That was the day I learned every curse word in Spanish."

I looked between Emery and Flirt. "Are one of you going to tell me what Devil did to get you all in trouble?"

Emery smiled. "It was winter, and the wind took out the power, leaving the whole compound pitch black. You couldn't even see the moon and stars for the clouds. Shakes, Dare's ol' lady, was watching us at their house while the dads—Dare, Roscoe, Payton—and a few of the other members and prospects, who lived on the compound at the time, started filling coolers with ice, making sure everyone's cabin and the clubhouse had enough wood for the fireplaces after the power had been out for a couple of hours. Shakes had their fireplace going, and we were in the living room playing games on the floor by the light from the fire and candles she'd lit around the room. Shakes curled up on the couch while she was watching us and fell asleep.

"Devil thought it would be funny to scare her. We agreed, but we couldn't think of anything until Devil mentioned a bearskin rug in the old storage shed behind the lodge. The old building was initially used to store extra furniture and stuff for the lodge and cabins. We'd been told to stay away from the place because it had deteriorated over the years and the dads were afraid it would collapse. Of course, we hadn't listened and one day Devil had gone in there, and the rest of us spread out as lookouts so he wouldn't get caught. He found an old bearskin rug that was probably at one time in front of the fireplace in the main room. So that night when he mentioned getting it, we snuck out of the house and went to the shed and picked up the rolled rug. We carried it back to Shakes and Dare's house. Bungee cords kept the rug rolled, so once the rug was in the living room, we went to each end and unfastened the cords. Then we started unrolling the rug.

"Shakes shifted on the couch, and we knew we had to hurry if we were going to pull the prank off. We flipped the last fold of the rug and two raccoons jumped out—we screamed, Shakes sat straight up on the couch, then she screamed because from the floor the bear's head was looking up at her. Our screams scared the raccoons, and they took off around the house. Within two minutes, the front door swings open, banging off the wall as Dare and the dads barreled through the doorway with their guns drawn." Emery laughed as he finished telling the story.

"Oh my God, you guys deserved to get spanked." I laughed and wiped at my eyes.

"The dads and Dare spent two hours with flashlights trying to find where the raccoons had run to," Flirt added. "Christ, they were mad."

I shivered, and Emery glanced down at me. "Let's get you in the house and off your feet, *cariño*. I promised you dinner."

Emery started leading us toward the backdoor of his house, and Flirt walked with us to cross the yard to his place.

"Enjoy your dinner, brother," Flirt said and snorted as Emery turned us toward the door. "And Mackenzie?"

"Yes." I looked over my shoulder.

"Told you," he said and continued walking toward his house as I frowned.

"Told me, what?" I questioned.

"That he'd come looking for you." I glared in Flirt's direction, only to lose sight of him in the darkness.

"By the way, brother, me and you need to have a talk," Emery said as he unlocked the door and pushed it open, not even turning his head in Flirt's direction. I wasn't sure Flirt was still close enough to have heard him until I heard him chuckle.

"Sure, man. But can you wait and thank me later? I'm heading to Whispering Nights."

"Weren't you considering dropping your membership?" Emery asked as he pushed his key in the lock.

"Yeah, but I came across a reason to postpone that decision for the time being."

"Good for you. You never know, maybe this will be the one." Emery pushed the door open.

"Not sure, but I'm enjoying finding out."

"I bet you are. Be safe, brother."

"Always," Flirt replied, then I heard a door close in the distance.

Emery used a hand at my back to lead me into his home ahead of him. "What's Whispering Nights?"

Emery closed the door. "A club."

"He's in a club already," I said and frowned.

Emery's lips twitched. "A BDSM club, *cariño*.

"Oh my God, I never would have guessed that with Flirt."

"Familiar with Doms?"

"Not only am I *not* familiar. Well, besides what I've read in books. If you would have asked me five minutes ago if I knew anyone who was, I would have said no."

Emery grinned. "Should they wear tags stating it?"

"You're enjoying this."

"Yes, but I can think of something I would enjoy a lot more."

"What?" I asked offhandedly as I looked around and took in my surroundings. The backdoor led into a large kitchen with an eat-in area off to one side.

When Emery didn't immediately reply, I turned back to face him. I'd never, ever had a man look at me the way he was. Desire filled his dark eyes. They mesmerized me. I probably should have questioned the sudden change in him, but I couldn't form the words to ask.

He reached out and grabbed my arms. "It very much involves you," he said and turned us, changing our positions.

When I opened my mouth to ask him what he was talking about, I didn't get the chance. My back hit the door, and he leaned in, capturing my mouth with his.

The man was potent and in control. I, on the other hand, was lost. Everything I swore to myself I didn't want had been a lie. As he devoured my mouth, I wondered why I wasted so much time avoiding the man. To experience kissing him would have been worth putting up with his arrogance alone.

I felt the loss as he broke the kiss and pulled me into his chest, resting his chin on the top of my head.

"Damn, I want you so bad, but I'm supposed to be cooking your food," he said as my face rested on his chest, and I could hear the rapid beat of his heart. The kiss affecting him as much as it had me.

"I'm suddenly no longer tired or hungry," I said a little breathlessly and still reeling from the kiss.

His hands slid from my arms down to the hem of my shirt. "I need to know if you want me to stop."

"I don't want you to stop." The words had no more than left my mouth when my shirt was over my head and tossed to the floor. He unhooked my bra, and it quickly followed the shirt. My pants were more of an issue. He stepped back and undid them and pushed them all the way down, only to be stopped by my shoes.

I giggled when he cursed, then pulled the shoes off my feet. Once he removed them, my pants along with my panties were stripped from me. There was something to be said about being naked while he was completely dressed.

Emery stood, then bent until we were face to face, leaving me to stare in his dark brown eyes, which were now more black than brown.

"*Cariño*, you are as close to perfection as any woman could be."

I reached out and ran my fingers through his black hair and closed the space between us until our lips met. I started the kiss, but Emery immediately took over and devoured me for a second time. It was the only word to describe how he demanded and thoroughly dominated the kiss, leaving me breathless. Neither of us could get enough. Our tongues dueled, and he ran his hands down my sides, reaching my hips. His roughened hands ran over my bare skin and left goosebumps trailing behind.

Emery slid his hands behind me and grabbed the cheeks of my butt, where he squeezed and caressed. When he lifted me up, I wrapped my legs around his waist and brought my scorching center in contact with the material of his jeans. My clit throbbed as I shifted to gain a better grip with my legs, encountering his very sizeable and hardened cock. I rolled my hips, and he groaned and pulled away, breaking the kiss.

So much reflected in his eyes. The want and desire for me had my stomach tightening. His nostrils flared, and his arms adjusted until only one held me up while his other hand moved between us, giving him the ability to reach the front of his pants and unzip them.

Emery's cock sprang free and laid between my legs. I felt the heat of its touch to my core. He thrust his hips forward and slid through my folds. I squeezed, and he groaned as I tightened around his length.

"I need to put you down to grab a condom."

I dropped my legs until my feet hit the floor and watched as he reached into his back pocket and pulled out his wallet. After he took a condom out, he tossed the wallet, ripped open the packet, and had the condom rolled down his length before I heard the plunk of the wallet hit the floor.

"Up," he said and lifted me, and I wrapped my legs around him again. "Say you're ready, Mac. I feel like I've waited a lifetime to have you."

For a split second, fear touched me as I realized how easy it would be to give this man anything he asked for. Then, as I looked into his eyes as he waited for me to answer, I knew he'd never ask for more than I was willing to give.

I'd wasted so much time dodging him because I was sure I didn't want or need the man who knew exactly what he wanted. Me.

"Please, take me," I whispered, then gasped when he dipped his head and bit my nipple, licking it with his tongue to ease the sting. "Emery." His name was the only thing I could get out of my mouth before I leaned my head back against the door and just felt.

"Damn, *cariño*, you're already wet for me," he whispered against my breast, and I nodded. "So wet, so ready. I don't know if I what to fuck you or taste you until you scream my name."

I'd never been talked to like he was doing, and boy, I had been missing out. The more he spoke, the wetter I became, and the bolder I felt. I knew my body wasn't curvaceous as a lot of women's bodies were. My body didn't even come close. But the way Emery touched and kissed mine made me feel as if I was the most voluptuous woman in the world.

"Why choose?" I panted boldly as he kissed his way up from my breasts. He bit my earlobe, then swirled his tongue around the outline of my ear.

"Ah, my *cariño's* greedy. I like it. But you're going to have to wait for my mouth because I've decided I want to feel you stretched around my cock."

Emery adjusted until his cock slid through my wetness and the head was at my entrance. With one movement of his hips, he pushed in to the hilt and my back arched, and my shoulders touched the door. He held still only long enough for me to adjust to his size and then pulled out and thrust in again.

I rolled my hips and flexed, tightening my core around him. His hands gripped me so hard I knew I would sport bruises, but it would be worth it for what I was feeling and experiencing with him.

"Damn it, you're so fuckin' tight. I'm not sure how long I can last."

I moaned as Emery picked up the pace. He pulled me down as he thrust up. As he continued to pound into me, the only things that could be heard in the room were my moans, his groans, and the slapping of skin on skin.

"I'm so close," I warned breathlessly.

"Me, too. Take us over, *cariño*."

I laid my forehead on his shoulder and reached between us and rubbed my swollen clit, matching the speed of his thrusts. I pinched my clit and bit down on his shoulder through his t-shirt as he slammed into me. His cock twitched inside me, and he filled me one last time before both our bodies shook as we climaxed together.

As we worked to level out our breaths, Emery wrapped his arms around me and turned, carrying me through his house to the stairs. Once we'd entered his room, he bent and laid me on his bed. I felt the loss of him as he slipped from inside me. He stood and then walked into the bathroom.

When he walked back into the bedroom, minus the condom, I watched as he pulled his shirt over his head and tossed it aside. The man was beautiful. His tan skin was smooth and stretched over an abundance of muscles. His nipples were a dark brown and perfect for licking, and the only hair was the trail from his belly button down.

"God, you're a beautiful man," I whispered.

"Back at you, *cariño*, except the man part," he said and grinned as he bent over and untied his boots, kicking them away. When he pushed his jeans down, revealing all of him, I took my first good look at him, completely naked. No man should look that good. His cock was long, thick, and I shamelessly watched as he grabbed hold of it and pumped his hand up and down its length. I licked my lips and then slid a hand down until I touched my clit. I circled it, then rubbed in sync with his motions.

"Fuck, that's hot, and you can do that later while I watch. Right now, I want a taste."

He moved to the bed, knocked my hand out of the way, and settled himself between my legs. Emery wasted no time, and before long, my back arched off the bed. My head bent back as I screamed through the orgasm. I wasn't sure I'd survive the man.

Emery took my body to heights I never believed possible. And I was positive most of the things he was doing to me weren't covered in any medical textbooks I'd read.

Hell, maybe I'd write one myself was the thought that briefly drifted through my mind before I lost all ability to think as he worked his way back up my body and filled me.

Chapter Ten

Coast

At the knock on the door, I slid the skillet off the burner and went to answer the front door. I opened the door, and after saying good morning to my dad, I waved for him to follow me.

"Coffee's made. Help yourself," I said and walked over to the stove to finish cooking the steak in the skillet.

"Didn't know if you were up or not, but I thought I'd stop and check."

"You've been out already this morning?" I glanced over my shoulder at my dad, who was fixing himself a cup of coffee.

"Thelma had to be at the diner," he answered, then looked over at me.

I lifted my brow, then turned back to flip the steak. "Okay."

"Nothing smartass to say?"

"Nope. Unless you stopped by to ask for some advice." I grinned. Knowing that would get him riled.

"Kiss my ass. Maybe you need me to give you some advice. Out of the two of us, I'm the only one getting laid."

I started laughing because in no way had my dad and I ever shared any information about women we bedded or mentioned that we had.

"Damn it, what the hell are you laughing at?"

I placed the steaks on a plate and then reached for the bowl of scrambled eggs and the skillet I set out to use for them. After I emptied the bowl into the skillet. I turned around.

"You, because you're worried I'm going to be upset over you seeing Thelma. Or are you seriously worried about Tank and Bull? Because first, I think it's great. Second, I know I teased you about Tank and Bull, but if they've got a problem with you and their mom, they'll have to go through me to get to you. And I got no problem beating sense into both their asses." I turned around and picked up the spatula and worked on the scrambled eggs.

"Love ya, son."

"Love you, old man," I said, then added. "But I hope you aren't planning to give me any siblings. Putting up with Tank and Bull will be bad enough."

My dad chuckled. "Thelma and I are both a little old for that."

"Just wanted to get that clarified." As I finished the eggs, the oven timer buzzed, and I shut it off, then grabbed a towel. I opened the oven and pulled out the pan of biscuits.

"Who's all the food for? And why are you in such a good mood this early?"

I turned, ready to answer my dad, but I didn't have to.

"I hope there's coffee. And whatever you're cooking smells wonderful. I'm starving," Mac said as she walked into the kitchen, then stopped.

I grinned at what she had on. My t-shirt was down to her knees, and she wore a pair of my sweats, which had to be rolled about five times at the waist to fit her. Her hair was sticking out in places, and damned if I didn't have to adjust myself for wanting her.

When I woke, I'd wanted nothing more than to wake her and have her again. But since I'd woken her twice during the night, I left her sleeping in my bed. I'd known she was tired, and since we'd both missed dinner, I pulled on my jeans after coming out of the bathroom and headed down to the kitchen. I'd planned to wake her after the food was done.

"Well, my questions got answered. The food and why you're in a good mood," my dad said in Spanish.

Mac's eyes widened when my dad spoke and her cheeks redden as she looked from me to him.

"Mackenzie, you've met my dad, right?" I asked and grabbed a cup and filled it with coffee.

"Umm… yes. It's good to see you again, Mr. Cortez." I laughed at the look on my old man's face when Mac answered in Spanish. It would be one I wasn't likely to forget for a long time.

My dad looked at me, then spoke to Mac. "Good to see you, too. And call me Cruz, sweetheart. I'm aware of my age, but it always makes me feel older when a gorgeous young woman uses mister," my dad said, continuing to speak in Spanish. And though he had an accent to begin with, I noticed it was slightly heavier than normal.

Mac grinned and continued to speak Spanish like he had. "Oh, like anyone would look at you and think old. From your looks, it's hard to believe you are old enough to have a son Emery's age." She might have told me she had a little difficulty sometimes, but the woman spoke fluently even if she didn't think so herself.

"Damned if you aren't good for a man's ego. If my son wasn't—"

"Alright, enough," I said, cutting my dad off. He and Mac both grinned, knowing why I'd done it. No man wanted to watch or hear their woman flirt with their dad. "Food is ready. Sit down at the table, *cariño*, and I'll bring the food over." I grabbed the plates with the food on them and set them on the table and went back for the biscuits.

"I can help. Just point where I can find the plates and silverware."

"Dad, are you staying? There's plenty."

"Nah, I'm going to head home," he said and headed to the sink to put his coffee cup in it.

"Oh please, stay and eat. There is no way we can eat all this," Mac said, and I watched my dad's eyes soften. I knew it wasn't that he didn't want to stay and eat. If it would have been one of the guys here, he wouldn't have thought twice about sitting down.

"If you're sure? I don't want to interrupt your and Emery's time together, more than I have."

"Why wouldn't I be sure? Not like we had plans to have sex on the table during breakfast."

I stared at Mac, and so did my dad. When she placed her hands on her face and groaned, we laughed.

"I can't believe I said that. I need more coffee."

"Sit, and I will get you more. Dad, can you get the plates and silverware while I grab a shirt?"

"Sure can."

Mac took a seat at the table as I walked out of the kitchen to get a clean shirt. When I walked back into the kitchen a few minutes later, Mac and my dad sat at the table talking. I noticed Mac already had another cup of coffee in front of her. I grabbed my cup off the counter and joined them at the table.

We filled our plates and talked while we ate. Well, I ate as my dad talked, and Mac laughed at the stories he told of some of the shit my brothers and I had done when we were younger.

As I watched Mac wipe the moisture from her eyes from laughing so hard, I wondered if she thought it would be rude if I hauled her out of the chair and told my dad to get out, so I could take my woman back to bed.

I looked over at my dad, and he grinned, then started in on another story. It was as if he knew what I'd just thought.

Well, as the saying 'start as you mean to go on' filtered through my mind, I pushed back my chair and stood. Then I moved to Mac and slid one arm under her legs and the other behind her and lifted her out of the chair.

I looked at my dad. "You need to go, and turn the lock as you go out the door."

"Oh my God, Emery. Put me down. You're so rude," she said along with a bunch of other stuff as I toted her through the house and started up the stairs.

"Nice talking with you, Mackenzie. I'm sure I'll see you around since my son finally pulled his head out of his ass," my dad yelled on his way out the door.

"I'll never be able to look your dad in the face again. I can't believe you." Mac was going on as I reached my room.

I tossed her on the bed and followed her down. It didn't take long before the ranting turned to moans.

I slid out from under Mac and reached over the side of the bed for my jeans. Pulling them off the floor, I snagged my cell out of the pocket and looked down at the screen and opened the text message and read it. I looked at the time on the phone, and the time the text came in.

"Damn."

"What's wrong?" Mac asked as she stretched.

"Nothing bad. I have Church in thirty minutes," I said and sat up on the side of the bed.

"Oh, I guess I could call an Uber. Will you have time to drop me off at the gate?" Mac sat up.

"Why the hell would you call an Uber?"

"Well, there isn't enough time for you to drive me to my car and then get back here in time for your meeting."

"Do you have to have your car right now or in the next couple of hours?"

"No, but if you drop me at home, you still won't make it back in time, and then I'm still going to need to get my car at the hospital."

I ran my hand down my face. "Let's start over. Do you have anything that needs to be done sooner than in a couple of hours?"

"No. Well, unless another of my pregnant patients goes into labor or I have an emergency with one of them."

"We can work with that. You can relax here while I'm at Church, then when I get back, we can go pick up your car. I'll follow you to your house and you can leave your car and pack a bag to stay here tonight. We can spend Sunday lying in bed and lounging around the entire day. Bar nothing happens with one of your expecting patients." I chuckled. "Four of your expecting patients live within walking distance of this house."

"Oh no, don't say that. They have months to go. Definitely don't want them going into labor for quite a while."

"Okay, poor attempt at a joke. But does everything else work for you?" I asked as I stood and walked around the bed.

"I can wait to get my car. But, Emery, I'm not sure about the rest. I mean, all this is happening so fast. Don't you think?"

"No. I've been drawn to you for months and months, and if I hadn't pushed, I'd still be trying to chase you down.

Sex with you is beyond explosive, but that isn't why I want you to stay again." One of Mac's eyebrows went up, and I chuckled, then continued. "Okay, let me rephrase that. I want sex with you again. Hell, I'll take it whenever I can get it from you, but it isn't the *entire reason* I want you to stay. I work during the week, so do you. Even weekends and nights when you must. I want to get to know you, and since I've waited forever to be with you. I don't want to spend just a couple of hours with you on the weekends or an hour or two here and there during the week."

"Okay."

"Okay, you'll stay for the rest of the weekend?"

She smiled. "Yes."

I reached for her arm and pulled her to her feet, then kissed the top of her head. "That's great. Now, let's take a shower."

"I thought you said you had thirty minutes until Church?" she asked as I walked us toward the bathroom.

"Yep, so quit dragging your feet, or you're going to make me late."

"Oh, no you don't. You're not blaming me for being late. I'll shower after you."

I tugged her behind me and into the bathroom. "I'm going to have you before I leave, but it will save time taking you in the shower. So if you want me to fuck you on the bed, then take a shower, I'm guaranteed to be late. If we're in the shower already, it will be close, but I should still make it in time. Which do you want?"

"The shower."

"My woman knows about utilizing time and saving water."

She giggled, and I kicked the door shut.

Chapter Eleven

Coast

I walked into Church, and five pairs of eyes looked at me. The five faces each wore a different smile.

"Well, look who decided to join us. Takes a week off, then saunters in all loose hipped," Jag said.

"Yeah, you'd think he'd be wearing a smile instead of a scowl," Devil added.

"Who wants to make a bet? I say he not only makes Mac an ol' lady. I got a hundred that says he'll take it all the way and be married by Christmas," Flirt said and chuckled when I flipped him off.

"I'll take that bet. But I say he won't wait around like some, and he'll have a ball and chain before Christmas," Jag said.

"Hey, Sami is the one who won't set up a time. I've got a ring on her finger. That counts," Speed said and glared at Jag.

"Carly's got my ring on her finger, too. She's my ol' lady, and that has just as much if not more meaning than a piece of paper," Crusher argued.

"Bailey wants to wait until the baby is born," Devil said.

"Fuck all of you. I'm going to take it slow with Mac. I don't want to push too hard and have to chase her down again," I said, and my brothers laughed.

"Yeah, I'm in on the bet. Coast being patient. That would be a first," Devil said, and he and Flirt bumped fist.

"Put me down for a hundred for before Halloween," Jag said.

"Me, too. Make mine before Thanksgiving. I'll give him a little time," Crusher said.

"Oh, shit. You need to marry her on Thanksgiving," Devil said and laughed. I frowned, and from my other brothers' faces, they were just as confused as I was.

"What the hell does Thanksgiving have to do with getting married?"

"Oh, come on, work with me. It would be cool as hell to have you get married before we have the club's big Thanksgiving dinner. You already have the part of the Indian covered, and Mac can wear a Pilgrim dress."

"Something is seriously wrong with you, Dev," Speed said and shook his head.

I shoved Devil as I sat in the seat beside him. "You're such a dumbass."

"You know it was a joke, right? 'Cause I love you, brother."

"Of course, I know it was a joke. You still got your hair, don't you?" I laughed, and so did the others.

"Hey. Why're you laughing at his scalping joke, and you didn't laugh at mine?" Devil asked and looked around the table.

"Because we weren't laughing at his joke. We were laughing, picturing you without hair," Flirt answered.

"No one touches the hair. Well, except Bailey when she grabs hold of it while I'm eat—"

"Stop!" Speed yelled and cut Devil off. "Have you been hanging around Roscoe?"

"No more than usual. Why?" Devil asked.

"Never mind. You have issues, brother," Speed said and shook his head again.

Devil shrugged. "Like you just figured that shit out."

I burst out laughing. Damn, I loved these men.

"Alright, let's see if we can get to some business before Ghost gets here and catches us up on the construction business. Flirt's already got the reports on the gym, pot store, and Soft Tails," Crusher said.

"Really? The pot store. Tell me in the few days River and I were gone, Boss and Turk did not fill out anything with that as the name."

"No, Jag. I just find it easier to call it what it is," Crusher answered.

"Thank fuck, because with Boss and Turk, anything is possible," Jag said, and I snorted. The way Boss and Tuck were, I imagined they smoked as much as they sold.

"Just us today?" I asked.

"Yeah. We'll have the full member Church at the first of the month as usual," Crusher said, then added. "I wanted us to go over a few things, so if we needed additional information, we'd have it together before the full club meeting."

"Sounds good, Prez," I said, referencing Crusher for his position in the club.

"Let's get this underway," Crusher said, then looked to Devil. "You don't have to keep the minutes since this is leadership only."

Devil gave a thumbs up, and Crusher rolled his eyes. The club had grown since we took over, which wasn't a reflection of our dads' reign. We'd added more businesses, and we'd brought on more prospects to help with the minor jobs no one had the time to deal with now.

The meeting started, and we went over the financial records of each business. The club was doing excellent overall. Even our custom bike shop. At the pace it was going, we would exceed our original profit margin goal by ten percent. The club was sustaining its income even with Soft Tails' stripping side closed temporarily. The bar side had picked up business once we'd opened it as a separate entity from the stripping. Seemed people in town loved Perry's cooking. Once the renovations were finished and the stripper side opened, profits would improve rapidly.

Roscoe's pawnshop was running steadily. It sold as much merchandise as it'd taken in over the last year. It was good to see. It meant the town was having a financial up year because fewer people needed cash and the easiest way to get it was to pawn something.

"Tank has worked out great managing Soft Tails. Luna helped him with lining up talent, and Sami spent time with him on the books. Not his favorite part of the job, but he's keeping up. We might have to get him help or an assistant if bringing in the showcase strippers bumps business. Tank can't sit in the office the whole time he's there. He needs to be on the floor. Just something we need to keep a watch on," Jag said.

"I wanted to bring something to the table and get your opinion. If you like the idea and think it would benefit the club, then we can put it on the agenda for a full club vote," Crusher said, then looked at each of us, and we nodded.

"Hit us with it. If it brings money to the club, we're all for it," Jag said.

"It pertains to Yoga Sensual," Crusher said and waited.

"What about it? As long as you aren't going to tell us we have to take classes there, I'm good," I said and noticed Jag and Devil were the only two who didn't nod in agreement.

"No one has to take classes. I don't even want to picture any of you on a yoga mat," Crusher answered.

"I don't know why it would bother you. We're in shape. Personally, I'd rock a pair of those pants," Devil said, and I turned my head and stared at him.

"Christ, what has gotten into you, brother?" I asked and shook my head. Devil had always been the jokester, the one who usually started the shit that got us in trouble growing up.

"I'll tell ya," Speed snickered from the other end of the table. "He and Jag are catching heat from Bailey and River. Willa started a class for pregnant women, and one woman said it would be nice if their husbands could join in. Yeah, Sami asked me if I would take a class. I won't go into what transpired after my 'fuck no' response, other than I had to explain to Ally the next morning why I was sleeping on the couch."

Crusher, Flirt, and I burst out laughing. "Laugh it up. Just wait, assholes, your time is coming. I've come across some vicious women, but pregnant women—their mood swings can go from murder to sweet in twenty minutes," Jag said.

"Yeah, brother. But on the other side of the hormone valley, I ain't going to complain about the sex," Devil said, and he and Jag bumped fist.

"If that's the case, I'm not sure I'll survive Carly in the pregnant state. My dick's raw from trying to get her pregnant," Crusher announced.

"Yo, brother. SISTER!" Speed said, then ran his hand down his face. "What you should be worried about is your kids if they take after her."

"You still upset over Ally?" Crusher asked Speed.

"What do you think? My kindergartner daughter gets in trouble at school for saying Karma is a bitch. Then I have Sami riding my ass about watching what gets said in front of

Ally. She gets shit from Carly, and I'm the one who pays the price," Speed griped.

"Dude, what are you complaining about? Do you know the shit I had to listen to after I told Bailey?"

"Would you rather they let some little punk ass kid bully them, instead of standing up and putting them in their place?" Flirt interjected, and I had to agree.

"Can't always be there to protect them. So at least you know they can take care of themselves. I already feel sorry for the men who step up thinking they can manage them." The glares directed at me had me smiling.

"Ally can date after I die," Speed said.

"Yeah, good luck with that." I grinned as he scowled.

"All the wooded property surrounding Black Hawk will come in handy. Because if any asshole thinks we'll stand back and let them at the daughters of Black Hawk…" Crusher said and left the rest of the sentence unfinished. He didn't need to finish it. Every man at the table and in the club would have no problem burying a body if a hair on any of the girls' heads was harmed.

Hell, I really felt sorry for the poor bastards. And it didn't escape me that somewhere out there were unsuspecting young boys who had no idea what the future held for them.

"Prez, we got off track. What did you want to ask about Yoga Sensual?" Flirt asked, bringing us back to business.

"Dad mentioned Willa might have to find a cheaper place to move into. Business is good, but not fluent enough for her to hire help. She wants to hire another instructor and doesn't have the cash flow to do it. Willa thinks if she moved to a cheaper place, she could swing the added cost. He brought it up because if she moves, we'll be out a tenant. Does anyone have a suggestion on either helping her or an idea for the space if she pulls out?" Crusher looked around the table.

Flirt raised his hand. "Hold up. How does Stroker know all about Willa's business?"

Crusher sighed. "He's seeing her. I didn't want to bring that up and have it be a factor in anyone's decision on what we should do."

"I'm going to play devil's advocate and ask. Is he seriously seeing her, or is she just the person he's fucking right now?" Jag asked.

Crusher ran his hand down his face. "Seriously seeing her. I'm not just saying that because he is my dad. He never has hidden any... conquest... for lack of a better word. I'm not sure he wouldn't be hiding the relationship if I hadn't gone to the place to pay for Carly's classes and caught him and Willa together."

"Another one of them down. I find it humorous every time I see my dad with Claire. But it is nice to see him relaxed and happy," Flirt said, and I had to agree with him.

"I couldn't agree more. It's a bonus to give them shit about it. But back to not thinking of your dad and Willa's relationship as being a factor. It is," I said, then added. "Club takes care of its own. We always have."

"Have Stroker ask Willa to hold off a bit. I'll run numbers. We might could do away with charging her rent. If we offer her clientele packages from our massage side. What we lose on her rent could be made back that way. The club wouldn't be out of anything except potential profits. Leaving us where we are right now." Flirt shrugged.

"Alright, run the numbers, Flirt. I'll have my dad talk to Willa. Anyone have an issue with looking at helping her?" Crusher asked.

"No, like Coast said. We take care of our own. If the numbers don't work out that way, then we find another way," Jag said, and the rest of us agreed.

"Okay then, now let's finish this up. Ghost should be here in five."

We'd just finished going over the last report when someone knocked. I got up and went to see who it was, and Ghost stood on the other side.

After a man hug, I asked him how he was doing.

"Great. They tell you I'm going to have two boys?"

"Devil did. Congratulations, brother," I said as he walked into the room.

"Thanks, brother."

"When we're done, if you're not in a hurry, I'd like to talk to you about the cost of windows and roofing material."

"You need work done at your place?" Ghost asked as he moved toward the table.

"Nah, it's for Kiyaya's place."

"Ah, that's your great granddad, right?" I nodded. "Then text me the measurements and number of windows, plus the square foot of the roof. If you know what type of windows, let me know. I'd suggest the ThermStar vinyl double hung. The price is competitive, and the window insulation is well-balanced for cold winters or the heat of summer."

"That will work. I have the information, so I'll send it to you. When you let me know the cost, I'll cut you a check. How long do you think it will take to get the windows in?"

"Should have them in a couple of weeks. The roofing material sooner."

"Great. Thanks, brother."

"Welcome. You going to need help installing them or laying the roof?"

"Dad will help me out. It's only seven windows. And the roof is just under a thousand square feet. Thanks for the offer, but I know you and Dare are working on a tight schedule."

"I can help," Flirt offered.

"I don't need to tell you any of us will help if you need us," Crusher said.

"I appreciate it. But with my dad and Flirt, we should be good."

"Just let us know," Jag said.

"Will do." I leaned back in my chair and looked at the brothers around the table. This was my family, and the only part missing for me was Mac. I knew my brothers thought I had no patience, which I didn't have an abundance, but I'd stretch what I had to take it slow with Mac. Her running was not an option. Especially after I'd touched and gotten a taste of her. Thinking of it made me wonder what Mac was doing at my house while she waited for me to get back.

I tuned back in when Ghost talked and listened as he filled us in on the progress with the remodeling of the gym and the massage side, which both would be ready to be opened at the end of next month. The pot store, or BHMC Dispensary, would be ready in two weeks and would open as soon as the final approval and license were received from the state.

As the meeting wound down, my eagerness rose. I couldn't wait to get back to Mac.

We all walked out together once the meeting ended. Ghost pointed at his truck. "You want to pile in? I figured you'd walked here since I didn't see any bikes when I drove up."

"Nah, brother. Go home to your woman, we're good," Flirt answered for us.

"I'm going your way. I have to pick Luna up. I dropped her at your house, Speed, but I'm sure she's at yours with the others by now," Ghost said and pointed to me.

"Why would they be at my house?" I asked, then it hit me. "Hell, how do they know Mac is at my house? When we rode in last night, it was dark, and no one was out. The only person who saw us was Flirt," I said and looked around at each of my brothers, then focused on Flirt.

"Wasn't me," Flirt said and held his hands up in surrender.

Ghost snorted. "I'm glad I live on the other side, but if the club ever falls short on cash, we could start a reality show like the Hollywood Wives and call it—The Women of Black Hawk."

Flirt laughed. "They don't miss much that's for sure. And, brother, I'm not even going to ask how you know about a show called Hollywood Wives."

"My bet would be on Bailey. You left right after she mentioned Mac was at the hospital because of an emergency." Devil shrugged when I looked at him.

"All I know is when I was outside unloading the back of my truck, Luna opened the door with her cell to her ear and asked if I would drop her off at Sami's on my way here. So that is what I did. When I pulled up in front of Speed's house, Carly was walking in. And no, I didn't ask Luna why she wanted to be dropped off. I've learned I'm better off not knowing," Ghost said, then glanced at each of us. "So, need a lift or not?"

The seven of us squeezed into Ghost's crew cab, and I was thankful it was a quick ride to my house. I only hoped Mac was still there, and the women hadn't freaked her out to the point she took off.

Chapter Twelve

Mac

The knocking at the door startled me, and I wondered if I should answer it. Emery had only been gone about forty-five minutes, and he would have his key, anyway. I walked to the door and looked down at the clean sweats and t-shirt I borrowed of Emery's after I'd taken a shower. His clothes hung off me.

Biting my lip, I reached for the lock.

"How long are you going to stand there before you open the door? I can hear you on the other side," Carly voiced from the other side of the door.

I'd been busted, and I had a feeling that when I opened the door, Carly wouldn't be the only one there. I took a deep breath, flipped the lock, and pulled opened the door. I was right; it wasn't just Carly outside. Bailey, Sami, Luna, and River stood on the porch with her. Neely, Ally, and Sawyer, who I knew was Dr. Agassi's daughter, stood looking at me while Poppy smiled from River's arms.

"Girl, are you going to let us in? I have to pee," Luna said, then pushed Carly out of the way. I stepped to the side, giving her room to move past me. Karma, the dog she and Ghost rescued, followed her. I hadn't even noticed the dog on the porch.

Recently, Luna had wrecked on her way to my office when a truck was in her lane as she came around a curve. The man had just thrown a trash bag out the window with Karma's puppies inside. When River's dad, the sheriff, went out to the man's house, he'd found the momma dog half-starved. Ghost and Luna had talked the shelter into letting them adopt the dog without going through the standard waiting period. They'd named the pitiful thing Karma and, from what I heard from Bailey, the dog had taken to Luna and rarely left the woman's side.

"Next time, ask me to move. And how can you pee again? You peed right before we left Sami's house," Carly said as the women walked inside.

"Sorry," Sami said and started walking down the hall. "I'm going to need to go after Luna finishes."

As I watched Sami walk down the hallway, I noticed Karma sat patiently by the bathroom door, waiting for Luna.

"I haven't seen Karma in a while. She's really filled out and looks great," I said as I turned to the other women.

"Yes, she looks great. Now let's go in the kitchen and sit down, and you can tell us how you ended up at Emery's house last night," Carly said, and Bailey smacked her shoulder.

"Can you be any ruder?" Bailey asked in a scolding voice.

"I know that's a rhetorical question because you know Carly is," River said, and Carly flipped both women off.

The little girls giggled, reminding us they were there, watching and listening.

"Carly," Bailey said, and I wanted to laugh at the look on Bailey's face but didn't want to draw her attention to me. She already had that mother warning look down pat.

"At it again," Luna said as she walked toward us.

Carly looked down at the three little girls. "Just because grownups do and say sh… stuff doesn't mean kids are allowed to do the same stuff. Got me?" Then she looked at Bailey. "Better?"

Bailey scowled at Carly but didn't have time to reply.

"Got it. Like when tell me not tell daddy when you say your brother needs to pull the stick out his butt, but not butt, the other word that is bad. The one you say and have to give me a dollar," Ally said just as Sami stepped out of the bathroom.

"Oh, really? What else does your aunt Carly tell you?" Sami asked Ally while she glared at Carly.

"Would anyone like something to drink?" I asked before Carly said something else to get herself in more trouble.

"Yes, that would be great," River said with a little more enthusiasm than needed, and if I had to guess, since she spent more time around the women, she too was trying to switch attention away from Carly.

I started toward the kitchen, and the women and kids followed. When Carly spoke, I couldn't help but grin. I was thinking the woman did and said things just to get the other women going.

"Are you sure neither of you have to go to the bathroom again since we're walking past it?" Carly asked. Once in the kitchen, she looked at me. "Being around the four of them pregnant is like a constant revolving bathroom door. One is always going in as another comes out. By the end of their pregnancies, I bet they will know where every restroom is located at the stores they frequent the most. I went with Sami to the grocery last week, and she went three times while we were there."

I chuckled and moved to the refrigerator. "I'm not sure what Emery has to drink," I said and pulled open the door. "Milk, beer, what looks to be a pitcher of tea, and some juice boxes," I told the women. Then I tried to picture Emery drinking from a juice box.

"The juice boxes are for us," Ally said, and I looked over to the door at her.

"That is sweet of him to keep you drinks at his house."

"Yep, and he keeps chocolate for us. Can we have some with our juice?" Neely asked as she moved to stand by Ally.

I smiled at the girls, thinking I might learn more about Emery from them instead of the women.

"If it's okay with your moms." I looked toward Bailey and Sami, and they nodded. "Okay, juice boxes and chocolate. You'll need to show me where Emery keeps your stash."

Ally and Neely walked over to the island, opened the cabinet underneath, and kneeled. I pulled three juices boxes from the fridge and set them on the counter, then water bottles for Sami, Bailey, Luna, and River.

I heard pans clanging together. "Need help?" I asked, and Ally's head popped out of the cabinet.

"Nope, got it. Uncle Coast puts it in the back inside a pot," Ally explained as she and Neely stood with a bag of candy. Then they closed the cabinet.

"Do you want to sit at the bar?"

"Can we go to the living room and watch TV?" Ally asked.

I looked over at Sami to see if it was okay. I did not know if Emery allowed the kids to eat in his living room.

Carly got up from the table and handed the bottles of water to the other women, then she held her hand out to Ally for the bag of candy.

"Give it up, shrimp. You each can have two pieces, then put the bag back. I'm a little annoyed. I didn't know about this stash. What else does Uncle Coast have stashed around here?"

"We'll never tell!" Ally and Neely yelled together.

"Hmm… keeping stuff from the cops."

I didn't know what to expect when I watched the smile form on Neely's face. The one she shared with her brother. But I bit my lip to keep from laughing when she looked up at Carly and said, "Dev says never admit shit to coppers."

"Oh, good grief, that man," Bailey said and laid her forehead on the table, not even bothering to say anything to Neely. I shouldn't, but I found it all amusing. It said so much about the men and the little girls' relationships.

Sami reached over and patted Bailey's back. "I share the same pain daily," Sami said, and River and Luna snickered.

"I'll help you get them set up in the living. Coast lets them eat and drink in there all the time. He doesn't worry about messes since Shakes, and a couple of the other ol' ladies clean the house." Carly grabbed up the juice boxes while the girls chose their candy.

"Why do they clean his house?"

"They used to do all the houses. Now they only do Flirt's and Coast's since we moved in with the other men. Shakes was so thrilled her baby boys were settling down, she wanted to help us with the cleaning, too," Carly said as we walked into the living room with the girls.

I hadn't paid much attention to the room before. It was laid out nicely with two couches across from each other and a loveseat separating them. In the middle of the u-shape of furniture was a square, overly large table. The furniture faced the fireplace with a flat screen mounted above it. Everything flowed together, and with the throw blankets on the back of the couches and throw pillows in each corner, it helped give the room a cozy feel.

With the girls settled and the TV on, we went back to the kitchen. Carly pulled the tea out while I grabbed the glasses. Once filled, we joined the other women at the table.

River handed Poppy her sippy cup. "I don't care that Shakes has spoiled those men. I'm thankful she and the other ol' ladies kept up with the houses. Dom is a slob. I cringe just thinking what his house would look like if the cleaning had been left up to him."

When River used the shortened version of Jag's given name, Dominic. Calling him Dom, it brought back something from the evening before. "What do you guys know about Whispering Nights?" I asked and didn't feel the least bit guilty of asking the women. I was curious.

"Ah, did you figure it out on your own?" Luna asked, then patted Karma's head when the dog stirred at her feet.

"What are you talking about?" River asked.

Carly shook her head. "Whispering Nights is the sex club Flirt goes to, to get his Dom on."

River blinked. "Get out! Well, that answers so much about him."

Luna looked at River and laughed. "Seriously. The first time I met the man, I knew. He might look as if he should be at the beach, catching waves on a surfboard, but his aura screams Dom. How can anyone not see that?"

"Probably because they don't have your hippie vision." Luna continued to laugh, unaffected by what Carly's reply.

"I knew. I thought everyone else did, too," Bailey said and shrugged.

"I didn't know until I overheard the guys talking one day and pieced it together," Sami said.

"Okay, enough about Flirt getting his BDSM freak on. I want to hear how Mac ended up at Coast's house," Carly said and cocked a brow as she looked at me.

"Oh, enough. There are times you don't need to know everything. I'm glad Coast wised up and went for it. He deserves to be happy and so do you, Mac. Whether or not it is with each other. I'm simply happy you are here now," Sami said.

"Thanks, Sami."

"Please, you all want to know the details, too. I just don't have time to beat around the bush. I'm not like some people who work Monday through Friday. I've got to go to work in two hours," Carly said.

"Evidently, the woman agreed to come. I don't see why you need the details," Sami said.

"I'm not sure I agreed," I said, then chuckled. "Yet here I am."

"I've been in your shoes, Mac. It doesn't take much to fall for one of these men. Our situations are similar. When I first met Dom, he came across as an arrogant ass from the start. We circled each other for months and tossed insults every time we crossed paths. The man got under my skin. Then he had to fly across the country to meet a daughter he didn't know about, and I went with him. I'm going to warn you, though. You'll never win against their dads. You can't say no to them. I ran into Flyboy, Dom's dad, in my car. It was before I even knew he was Dom's dad. We argued on the street in front of the bakery. Anyway, when the man asked me to help his son, and I saw the pleading in his eyes. I knew I was in trouble. How those men have gotten to their age without a woman latching onto them is amazing to me. They can be gruff, controlling, and a little scary when you meet them. But what you can't deny about them is they love their sons and would and will do anything for them. Even pleading for someone to help them. And the men are just like their dads.

"What I'm trying to say, Mac, is don't put a time on falling in love because you might just miss out on something special. I almost did. If you feel anything for Coast, give him a chance, you won't be disappointed," River finished, and I hadn't even noticed how quiet the room had gotten while she spoke.

"Well, I'm going to add congratulations because the man is fine. His dark looks make him seem mysterious and dangerous, and who doesn't like those qualities in a man," Luna said.

"Does Ghost know you think Coast is fine?" Carly looked at Luna and lifted her brows.

"Brax knows he doesn't have to worry. I'm carrying his sons. Besides, I've loved the man my entire life," Luna said.

These women made it sound so easy to love one of these men. Could it really be that easy? And could I take the leap to explore the possibility with Emery? I was brought out of my inner debate when Bailey asked if I wanted to go shopping with them the next weekend for baby things.

"I'd love to. It will be fun," I answered.

Before anyone else could say anything, Karma stood and walked out of the kitchen.

"Well, our impromptu party is about to be crashed. Karma can hear her daddy's truck, and you know he won't be alone," Luna said and stood.

"I don't hear anything," I said.

Luna held up a finger. "Give it a second."

Sure enough, I could hear a truck engine growing louder as it got closer.

The rest of the women stood, and we walked out of the kitchen. Sami and Bailey headed for the living room where Ally, Neely, and Sawyer sat watching TV.

No sooner than the sound of the engine died I heard several doors slam, then the front door opened, and Emery walked in with the other six men behind him.

"You're still here," he said as he walked toward me.

"And why wouldn't I be?" I asked.

Emery pointed over his shoulder with his thumb. "That bunch," was all he said before he pulled me into his arms and kissed me until my head swam. The clearing of a throat brought me back, and I realized we stood in the entrance to a living room filled with people.

I shoved against Emery's chest until he released me and stepped back.

"Dam… dang, brother, give us a minute to round up the women and kids and we'll get out of here," Devil said, and the other men chuckled.

I felt the heat rise on my face. "No sense in getting embarrassed, Mac. Not much stays private with this bunch," Flirt said as he stood by the front door. He was the only the man who hadn't walked entirely into the house.

When I looked at him, I realized if I was going to be around these men, I needed to hold my own.

"I found out today that evidently, there are some things that stay private around here," I said and jumped when Flirt threw back his head and laughed. The women stood with their mouths open, while the men behind them had smiles on their faces. I had to admit, I worried I'd overstepped until I looked up at Emery and he winked.

Flirt recovered and looked at me. "That there is, Mac." Then he turned his gaze toward Emery. "Happy for you, brother."

The women and men, with the kids leading the way, started walking toward the door. I watched Dr. Agassi's daughter stop beside Flirt and look up.

"Who do you belong to?" she asked.

I shamelessly watched Flirt's reaction to Sawyer's question. And when I looked over at the other women, their eyes were on the two also, so were the men's.

I saw Flirt's brow crease when he looked down at the little girl. "Who do you belong to?"

"I asked first."

"Come on, Sawyer. Let's get back to the house," Sami said and moved closer to the door, putting one hand on Ally's shoulder and the other on Sawyer's.

"He don't belong to anyone. That's my uncle Flirt," Ally told Sawyer.

"What's wrong with you? Are you one of those men who is interested in younger women? Or one who don't have a job?"

The little girl was something else and, unlike me when I'd first met the men, wasn't the least bit intimidated.

The men chuckled, and I watched Flirt's lips twitch. "Ah, you're the interrogator?"

"What's that?"

"Yep, that is Sawyer, the ped's daughter," Devil interjected.

"The doctor in the building next to Mac's?" Flirt asked.

"Yes, her pediatric practice is next to mine," I answered. Puzzled when Flirt grinned down at Sawyer.

"To answer your questions, Sawyer. I don't belong to anyone. But I'm hoping to take care of that soon. And there's nothing wrong with me. Plus, I have a job."

"That's good. Women want those things. You're pretty, too. Everybody needs someone. My mom does. She don't have a husband."

"Well, now I understand why she and Ally hit it off. Let's go," Speed said, chuckling while reaching for the door.

After everyone walked out and the door closed behind them, I looked at Emery. "What just happened here?"

"Family, *cariño*." Was the answer I got from Emery before I was lifted into his arms and carried upstairs.

Needless to say, we never made it to the hospital to get my car. Or to my house for clothes.

Chapter Thirteen

Coast

"Fuck!" I yelled, reached up, and moved the hand from my face.

"What's wrong?" Mac asked sleepily as I touched my nose and expected to see blood when I pulled my hand away.

"Oh, nothing. I enjoy being woken out of a dead sleep by a smack to my face."

The bed shook as Mac giggled. "Sorry. When I'm overly tired, I sometimes thrash around in bed."

"And you find this funny?"

"Ah, poor baby," she said, then shifted until her face was above mine. "Let me kiss it and make it better." She leaned in and started peppering my face with kisses.

"Hell, if I'd known you were going to do that, I would have said you hit me on the dick." I chuckled, then flinched. "Ouch. No need to twist my nipple, *cariño*."

She moved, kissed the nipple she'd twisted, and started giggling again. I smiled, enjoying the playful side of Mac. A lot. But her playfulness had me hardening, so I pushed her onto her back and had her under me with my mouth taking hers before she could react.

I ran my tongue over the seam of her lips, and when she opened, I pushed my tongue in. I broke the kiss, only to bury my face between her neck and shoulder while I gained my breath. Her breaths came just as hard. Her breasts raised with each one she took, and her nipples grazed my chest.

Raising my head, I trailed kisses down her neck, then across her collarbone and down until I reached her breasts. I circled her nipple with my tongue and bit gently as I pinched the other nipple between two fingers.

Her nails dug into my back, and she moaned. When her back arched, I knew she enjoyed what I was doing to her.

My cock throbbed between us, impatient for the wet warmth it would find. Having Mac like this would never grow old. I wanted so badly to spread her wide and sink into her, but she deserved so much more. So, I continued my journey down, kissing down her stomach and across to each of her hips. Her hands released my back only to grab onto my hair as if to guide me where she needed me.

"Relax. I'll get there." I kissed the top of her mound.

"Easy for you to say."

I smiled as I slid my hands down her body until I reached her thighs. I spread her wide and wasted no time as my tongue snaked out, and I licked her from back to front.

My groans and her moans were the only sounds in the room until I pushed my tongue through her folds, causing her back to arch and her nails to pierce my scalp.

"Emery!" she screamed when I pushed down on her clit with my tongue. Then I circled the nub with the tip of my tongue and sucked while I pushed a finger inside her. I felt her thighs tremble against my cheeks. "More, I need more."

I added a finger into her depths and pumped in and out. When I used my teeth to bite down gently on her clit, her body shook as the orgasm took hold. I used my fingers and helped her ride out the tremors, and when her body became lax, I began my journey back up her body. When I reached her lips, she opened and allowed me to share her taste with her.

One arm held my weight as I reached down with the other hand and grasped my aching cock. I ran it through her wetness, and when the head of my cock rested against her entrance, and I felt her heat, it hit me that in my rush to get to her; I hadn't grabbed a condom. She moved her hands over my hair as I groaned and laid my forehead on her chest.

"What's the matter?" she asked as her hands continued to move down until they rested on the back of my neck.

"I need to grab a condom, and I'm trying hard not to shoot my load before I enter you."

Mac blinked, and her eyes filled. I rolled until she was on top of me.

"*Cariño?*" Unsure why she suddenly had tears in her eyes. "Talk to me."

She shook her head, pushed up and off me until she kneeled on the bed beside me. I watched as she swiped at her cheeks, then took a deep breath and let it out slowly. When she looked at me, I could see the pain in her eyes.

"You can tell me anything, Mac."

"I never planned to be in this position. But goddammit, you had to push me. When I avoided you, I didn't do it, so you would chase me. I ran in the opposite direction and hoped you'd tire of the chase and lose interest because I didn't want to be here." She pointed at the bed.

I didn't respond, but I ran a hand over my chest where my heart was. I stared at the woman who kneeled naked on my bed. The woman who, for the last thirty-six hours or so, felt the pull between us as I did. I'd always been able to read people, but I'd blown it with Mac. I'd read her completely wrong.

I dropped my eyes from her face and prepared to move her and get out of the bed. My plan was to get dressed and take her home. Before I could rise, she clasped my forearm.

"Don't act hurt or pissed. You're responsible for it."

"And I'll correct it if you let go. We can get dressed, and I'll drive you home."

"Oh no, you won't."

"Excuse me," I said, confused about what the woman wanted. She didn't want to be here, but she wasn't going to let me take her home.

"It's too late now. You wormed your arrogant ass under my skin. I was fine on my own, then you sat beside me in the diner. My first thought was I'm not sure I'm strong enough to resist him. Then you got butthurt when I mentioned I could pay for my lunch. I decided then that I'd been confused about what I felt.

"But you wouldn't leave me alone. Every time I turned around; there you were. Don't get me wrong, I knew we'd run into each other because I had no intention of losing the friendships I've made with the women. I was doing good, too, until Jag and River's reception. You had to be sweet and attentive. And when your hand touched me, I felt it to my core. No one has ever made me feel that way. Being in your arms when we danced had felt fantastic and right, as if I were always meant to be there.

"That was the minute for me. The minute I knew it wouldn't be just a roll in bed to scratch an itch. Then I had to leave, and you were gone. I found myself glancing around for you and thinking of you at the odds of times. I wish I could say it was only when I saw the others together, but it wasn't. I'd go to the grocery, and I'd wonder what aisle I'd run into you on. You have driven me crazy. But once you find out that I can't give you everything, you'll change your mind, and I'll be left with the memory of you to remind me no man could ever want me. Not for the long haul."

"Damn it, woman. I'm more confused now. Why wouldn't a man want you long haul? Seriously? Fuck, *I* want you, and the last time I looked in the mirror, I'm a man."

153

"I'll never be able to give you or any man a family. I can't have kids, Emery. And it may be shitty on my part to want it all, but I do. I've always achieved and obtained everything I wanted. I've never failed, Emery. I wanted to be a doctor. I wanted to meet and fall in love with a man. I wanted to have children. Then bam, I ran straight into a wall, and it was taken away from me in a blink of the eyes.

"And the worst part is, it is my fault I can't have children. I was on track to becoming a trauma surgeon. The hours were grueling and long, and there was so much to learn. I started experiencing cramps, then it progressed into a sharp pain in my side. At least the pain felt like it was on my side. I put off going to the doctor and getting it checked out. I had too much to do and didn't want to take the time. How stupid was that? I was going to be a doctor and ignored every sign my body was giving because I was *too* busy. It's one of the first things I tell my patients. Listen to what your body is telling you. What a fraud I am.

"After a while, I started bleeding, leaving me no choice but to get checked out. I went to the ER, and they did their thing. Tests, bloodwork, eventually a biopsy. The next thing I know, a surgeon is discussing my options. A partial hysterectomy versus a complete. Surgery sooner rather than later. By the way, it could have been avoided if I'd come in when the cramping started.

"So, at twenty-three, I had a complete hysterectomy. If I'd gone to the doctor sooner, they would have biopsied one cyst from the one ovary where it started, and then they would have removed the one ovary when the test came back with cancer cells present. Instead, the cyst essentially popped, letting the cancer inside free. The bleeding was because the cancer moved into the inside wall of my uterus.

"I had the surgery. After I recovered, I changed from wanting to be a trauma surgeon to an OB/GYN, specializing in high-risk pregnancies. I figured if I couldn't have kids, then I'd guarantee others could. I could have a practice geared toward high-risk only, but I didn't want my days to be filled with some ups and a lot of downs. Nothing is worse for parents than to do everything right and lose the baby in the end. And as doctors, we might not show it, but the losses affect us, too. I decided to split my skills and have a little of the normal with no problems pregnancies, to yearly exams, to I will do anything required to have a baby, patients. Switching specialties, I get to experience bringing a new life into the world, just never as a mother. I've accepted that, but it doesn't mean I should keep someone else from experiencing it."

I grabbed Mac, and once she straddled me, I moved my hands to cup her face. "I'm sorry for everything you went through. But the months I've spent popping up where you were had nothing to do with your ability to give me children or not. It was all you. When I saw you for the first time, I wanted you and you alone. I was drawn to you. You are who I want to get to know better. I planned to take things slow with you, but you can blame yourself if I don't stick to that plan. And if you try to run, I'll catch you and remind you what you said about me being under your skin.

"You're smart enough to know you don't have to give birth to a child for one to be yours. Family isn't always about blood. Hell, my mother didn't have one ounce of maternal instinct inside her. Neither did my brothers' mothers. Blood nor the ability to pop out a kid means shit if you don't have anything to offer from here." I laid a hand over her heart.

Mac placed one of her hands over mine. "Maybe you aren't as arrogant as I thought."

My lip twitched. "*As* arrogant, huh? Well, are we going to see where this leads us?" I asked and turned my hand over and squeezed hers.

"I guess so." She squeezed my hand back and then started to slide off me. "Since my crazy killed the mood, we might as well get up."

I grabbed her waist and tossed her to the bed. "Yeah, I don't think so. I think we need to start over. The best part is, I won't have to stop and get a condom," I said, then started back at the beginning by taking her mouth with mine.

I had news for Mackenzie Minton, but I'd wait to share it with her. She said no man could ever want her. Did she not see what I did when she looked in the mirror? I knew there was a flaw in her reasoning. But no man would ever get the chance with her now—she was mine. And I protected and kept what belonged to me. Which included her.

We'd reached the point where we'd left off, and instead of reaching for a condom, I lifted to my elbows so I could watch her face as I moved my hips forward. I breached her entrance with one thrust and seated myself until I filled her fully.

"Christ, you're tight. I don't know how long I'll last," I said as I pulled back and pushed in. Her hips lifted to meet my downward thrusts until we set a pace that had us both on the brink. I felt my balls draw up and knew I wasn't going to last much longer, so I slid a hand between us, pressed down on her clit as I slammed in one last time and sent us both over the edge. We rode out the trembling of our bodies together. When our bodies and breathing settled, I pulled out and fell to her side, pulling her into my arms.

"I've never gone without a condom, so I didn't know if sex would feel different or not without one. I'm never wearing latex again because nothing could compare to you bare." I shut my eyes and sighed.

"I'm not sure whether or not it makes a difference, either. In the medical field, sometimes a test is run again and again to compare results before coming to a conclusion," Mac said, then laughed as I tickled her.

"You okay now, *cariño*?"

She snuggled closer. "Yes. Nothing like letting your inner lunatic out to cleanse your soul. But you know what's crazy? In my head, I know giving birth isn't the only way to become a mom. There are hundreds of kids waiting for a home. It's one reason after I settled here, I applied to become a foster parent. I'm not sure why I haven't actively started taking in kids, it just always seems like the wrong time. Maybe I'll check back in with DCYF. The Department of Children, Youth, and Families told me to let them know when I was ready, and they would activate me in the system."

"You're qualified as a foster parent?"

"Yes. The process took a little time, from the application to them checking me out and the in-house inspections. Plus, I had to go through a training course."

"I'd think being a doctor would have made the process easier for you."

"Nope, a doctor does not automatically make me parent material. Plus, I'm single and have a busy practice, so any children I foster who aren't school age would have to spend the day in daycare. Not to mention having a babysitter on-call for when I'm called to the hospital for middle of the night deliveries. Maybe it's what's held me back from becoming active. I hate thinking of a child spending all day in daycare."

When Mac mentioned being a foster parent, it made my thoughts go to Tracker and Paxton, and I wondered if they were doing better and if Mrs. Stone had gotten them into a home together.

"You asleep?" Mac asked and bent her head back so she could see my face.

"As you can see, no. But I am hungry." I moved and pulled us both up into a sitting position. "Come on, once we have breakfast ready, we can eat it on the couch, then lie around and watch movies. I'll even let you pick the first one."

"Oh my, you're too good for me. I'm swooning," Mac said, then yelped when I pinched her butt as she shifted and got off the bed and straight into the bathroom.

I grinned, pulled on my jeans, and headed downstairs. I'd use the bathroom off the kitchen, then get the coffee started. I was looking forward to spending the entire day with Mac. Hopefully, with no interruptions.

Sunday flew by, and it had been the most relaxing day I'd spent in a long time. And with no interruptions. Which was surprising, considering my brothers were home, too.

Mac and I cooked and ate. We watched movies, laughed, and talked about family. She told me about how her parents died and about her brother, who was in the army. I told her about Kiyaya, and how I'd ended up with my dad. I shared about my time in the military. She shared about her time in college and working hard in medical school. Which brought more questions from me.

"Did you start college at twelve? I know the training takes time. Not to mention you switched fields in the middle. No way you're older than thirty." Mac couldn't be past thirty, and if she were, it was barely.

She sighed. "I started college at fourteen and was in medical school before I'd turned seventeen. You know it isn't nice to ask a woman her age? I'm thirty-two."

"Wow, Mac. That's impressive."

"Thanks. At least you aren't looking at me like I'm a freak," she admitted, then her cheeks turned pink.

"I'm in awe of you, *cariño*. You accomplished things at an early age when most are just figuring out what they want to do with their lives. You should never get embarrassed by your intelligence. I'm proud of you for knowing exactly what you wanted and going after it. And if people looked at you as a freak, that's on them. They were jealous."

"It bothered me at first when I had no difficulty passing exams and some others with years on me failed. After years of being the youngest in every grade, though, I hate to say it, I became used to the looks and whispers. I just focused on getting through it all."

"You did it and then some." I kissed her and changed the subject because she seemed uncomfortable talking about it. It didn't help that I wanted to go back and beat the crap out of anyone who made her feel less because they had a problem competing with someone younger than them.

After we finished talking, I worked to blank out her mind with a heated necking session on the couch. Other than the sex that morning, we'd spent the day getting to know each other. I'd experienced nothing close to what Mac and I had done all day. I didn't want it to end.

"I need to go in. It's after eleven," Mac breathed out as I kissed her neck, then worked up to her ear.

"If you had let me come inside when we got here, you'd already be in bed," I whispered in her ear, then nipped the lobe.

"I told you when we were at the hospital picking up my car that you didn't need to follow me home. Now look at what your stubbornness has done. You've kept me on the porch for thirty minutes. If I had let you in, I still wouldn't be asleep. That is why you are on the porch and not crossing through the doorway. And didn't we decide to treat this as a normal dating situation? We agreed we wouldn't spend every night together?"

"You decided that. I remember saying I would stay at your place Sunday night through Thursday night and make the drive to Black Hawk since you work in town. You would then come to Black Hawk and stay with me Friday and Saturday nights."

"We can't spend every minute together. Trust me, you would be sick of me inside a month."

"Not a chance. And we wouldn't be with each other every minute because you work during the week, and so do I. What did you misinterpret today when I said I enjoyed getting to hold you? I'm trying to go slow, Mac, but everything in me wants to push you hard."

Mac chuckled. "If you can't be separated from me, what are you going to do next weekend when I go shopping with Bailey and the others?"

"I'm going to sit in my house and pout."

"Oh, I'd love to see that."

"Don't go shopping Saturday and I'll pout just for you. I'll even pout while I'm going down on—"

"Stop, stop, stop," Mac protested, laughing and cutting me off as she smacked my arm.

"Fine, I'll go so you can go inside your empty house and get into your cold bed. *After* you give me a goodnight

161

kiss. I hear couples who are *dating* do that," I said, and Mac sighed.

"One more kiss, then you'll let me go inside. Promise?"

"I promise."

"Alright."

Twenty minutes later, the door slammed on Mac's condo, and I listened as the locks clicked. The smile stayed on my face the entire way back to Black Hawk. Maybe the dating shit wouldn't be that bad after all.

Chapter Fourteen

Mac

"I really had fun. Thanks for inviting me along," I said as we pulled up at Sami's house.

"It was fun, but I'm not sure Kane is going to see it that way when I tell him how much I spent," Sami said as she parked the Expedition.

"Please. I was buying for two. I'm hiding the sales slips. No sense having Brax flipping out," Luna said as she opened the door and slid from the seat to the ground, then hit the handle on the side, so the seat leaned forward to allow Carly and I to get out of the third row.

"After seeing how much you four spent on the kids, I'm a little less eager to get pregnant," Carly said as she jumped down out of the vehicle. I followed her, but not as gracefully and easily as she had. Height definitely was a factor in the big SUV for short people. My height had been the deciding factor when I'd purchased a smaller SUV.

"Since I don't have to worry about spending money on kids, it was fun to help you ladies spend your money." With the day's shopping trip focused on kids and the upcoming babies, I'd been asked if I wanted kids or did seeing women go through labor regularly curtail that desire. I shared with the women the same talk I'd had with Emery. Minus my insecurities.

They told me how sorry they were. They'd said the same as Emery had. That I didn't need to give birth to a child to be a mom. Then the subject was dropped, and everything was the same as before. They'd treated me no differently. I'd been thankful for that because I hadn't wanted the women to feel as if they needed to walk on eggshells or avoid any future talk about babies around me.

"I'm blaming every cent I spent today on you, Mac. I don't even know the sex yet. Why did I let you talk me into buying so much?" Bailey said, and I chuckled.

"Yeah, I'm with Bailey. Poppy can never wear all the stuff I bought her before she grows out of it. Half of them came from you digging through the racks and finding more cute things. And I can't even explain the four bags of stuff for the baby who won't be born for months," River griped.

"Don't blame me. But I suggest if you ladies ever ask me to go shopping again that we take two vehicles. The extra truck space would come in handy, and I won't have to worry about climbing in or falling on my face getting out of the vehicle," I said as I held onto the back of the seat and the door's frame and lowered myself until my feet hit the ground.

"*If* we ask you to go again? Why wouldn't we?" Bailey asked as she lifted the backdoor where the bags were stashed.

"Because Emery and I may not work out, and though I know we're friends, he's your family. I wouldn't want it to be awkward for anyone." I shrugged, and all five women stopped and stared at me, then laughed.

Luna composed herself first. "You've been around the men for months. Have you not noticed they do nothing they don't want to do? I've seen Coast look at you, and, girl, he wants you."

"There are different wants. I'm not naïve. Men may think they want you, then after the chase and they spend time with you, they change their minds," I said and reached for a bag and was told to leave them that the men would get them.

"We've had this discussion. Besides, I got fifty dollars riding on you and Coast," Carly admitted, then laughed. Probably from my facial expression.

"Hey, I didn't get asked if I wanted to bet. And what does the bet entail between the two of them?" Luna inquired and placed her hands on her hips.

With Sami, Luna, Bailey, and River standing in a row facing Carly, they looked like a graph showing the different stages of pregnancy.

"The bet is when you think they will be married—like Halloween, Christmas, New Year's… They discussed it at the meeting, and Crusher told me about it. No way I wasn't betting," Carly answered Luna as I stared at her in disbelief.

"There are bets on when Emery and I will be married? Are the men insane? We've only been dating for a week!"

"Dating? Is that what you call it?" Bailey challenged and snickered.

"Yes. We are getting to know each other and taking it slow. I hate to inform you, but you wasted your money, Carly."

"First, we aren't crazy. Well, at least some of us aren't," Bailey said and looked to first Luna, then Carly. "Second, Coast has been vocal about what he wants. He won't settle for anything less, and what he wants is you, my friend. Because he sure isn't looking at anyone else and he acts like a man on a mission," Bailey finished and pointed behind me.

The men headed in our direction from Carly and Crusher's house. The only one missing was Flirt. When I looked at Emery, Bailey was right; his eyes were on me.

"Better tell her bye now, ladies. 'Cause he doesn't have the face of a man who is going to stand around chit-chatting," Luna said and laughed.

When the men reached us, Emery didn't even say a word until he lifted me up and started toward his house. He ignored my protest of his behavior but yelled over his shoulder about if I had bags in the truck, he'd get them later. Then he marched us into his house and up the stairs to his room. Instead of saying how much he missed me. He showed me.

It was a glorious end to the first week of being a couple.

In week two of the so-called 'dating' to get to know each other, I waited for Emery to step back. Instead, he stepped up to show me the man behind the rough exterior. The side of him he shared with me and no one else.

Like him taking the time in the middle of his day to ride into town and drop off lunch because I mentioned the day before I had a full schedule and wouldn't be able to even go out and grab something.

Or the day he picked up my car and took it to the garage to have the oil changed I'd put off for months. My car not only received an oil change, but it was also tuned up, cleaned, the gas tank was full, and it sported four new tires.

When I asked, "Why he had done all that?"

He replied, "Because it's my job to make sure you're safe. Not only with me, but when you are away from me."

As the end of week two ended, it was the understanding he'd shown when I was called away from the intimate dinner he'd planned and cooked, when I knew there was no turning back.

Into week three, we had the schedule of whose place we stayed at down pat. My apprehension about spending so much time together dissolved. I found as each day passed; we grew closer. I wasn't sure if I could sleep alone again if something happened to us.

It was too early to say the words, and I liked we didn't feel the need to blurt out things since our relationship had just began to blossom.

I'd never been in love and wondered if I'd know when it happened.

Chapter Fifteen

Mac

I unlocked my door and hurried inside my house. When I'd seen the last patient of the day, I'd closed the office an hour early, then stopped by the grocery store and picked up the ingredients for dinner. Nothing special—fried chicken, mashed potatoes, and vegetables.

After changing clothes, I headed to the kitchen to get everything started. During the week, our evenings were filled with cooking, eating, and if I were lucky, I'd last through the news as we cuddled on the couch. Then we'd go to bed and repeat it the next day. Emery had not complained once in over a month together about driving back and forth between my house and Black Hawk.

I'd noticed that morning after he left and I dressed, there were signs of him throughout my home. A t-shirt in my bedroom. A pair of jeans hanging in the closet. Even an extra pair of boots on the closet floor. The bathroom counter held his personal items, and his shampoo bottle was next to mine in the shower. The next time I went to his house, I would look for the signs of my presence. We'd become a part of each other's lives easily.

With a check on the time, I set the table. Emery would be on his way. I walked back to the stove, flipped the chicken, and turned off the burner under the pot of cooked potatoes. All normal things.

My cell phone rang, and I reached for it, swiping the screen, and holding it to my ear as I said hello. One phone call. Fifteen minutes in time. And the realization of how unfair life could be—struck me hard.

After I disconnected the call with my brother, Dirk, I turned the burn off to the half-cooked chicken and sat in one of the chairs at my table and placed my face in my hands and cried. When Emery walked in, that's how he found me. He lifted me from the chair, then sat down with me cradled in his arms.

"What's wrong, *cariño?*" he asked.

"Life is unpredictable and unfair. As a doctor, I know because I've witnessed it. But somehow, I've always been unable to separate myself when it pertains to me."

"Mac, I don't understand. What are you talking about?"

"Dirk called."

"Your brother, who is in the Army?"

"Yes. He called to tell me he was injured in Afghanistan," I said, then lifted my head and looked at Emery. "He lost part of his leg. They airlifted him to the U.S.

Combat Hospital on the Forward Operational Base. Stabilized him there, then sent him to Landstuhl, Germany. He's currently in Maryland at Walter Reed. I told him I would refer my patients to another doctor and fly to be with him. He told me no. He didn't want or need me uprooting my life to babysit him."

"I'm sorry, Mac. I'm surprised you weren't notified when he was first injured."

"Dirk told them not to. Damn it, Emery, why would he do that? Why doesn't he want me there? He's going to have an adjustment period. He'll need help. I'm his sister, for Christ's sake. I yelled at him, and we argued. My brother is in the hospital, recovering from a devastating injury, and I fight with him on the phone." I rubbed my eyes. They stung from crying.

"He needs time, Mac. And you can't take him not wanting you there personally. Dirk's going to need to work through things. You told me he was in for the long haul with the Army. His injury changed that. You may not have thought of it, but I guarantee he has. As far as not wanting you there. He's your big brother, Mac. He doesn't want you to see him at his weakness moment. He also knows you are building a practice and knows you'd give it up for him and he doesn't want to be the reason for it. He called you, *cariño*, he isn't trying to shut you out."

I knew there was truth to what Emery said, but it stung Dirk hadn't wanted me there.

After several minutes of quiet and absorbing Emery's warmth, I said, "Dinner's probably ruined."

171

"I bet we can salvage it together. What do you say?"

"Okay. We can always order pizza if it turns out nasty," I proposed as I slid off Emery's lap. He stood, then kissed my forehead.

"You going to be okay?"

"Yeah, I just had to have my freak out time."

"You can freak out anytime you have the need. I'll always be there to help you through it."

I stared at Emery long enough before he said my name as a question. "Mac?"

"Have you ever heard that a tragedy can bring people together?"

"Yes."

"I wondered if I'd know when it happened." Emery frowned at my words. I knew he didn't understand what was going through my head.

"Know when what happened?"

"When I fell in love. I love you, Emery Cortez."

His lips curled into a smile. "Ah, *cariño*, I'm glad you figured it out because I love you."

After a long kiss and the sound of my stomach growling, the moment was broken, and we went to work on getting dinner finished.

Life was unpredictable and unfair. I hadn't realized until I glanced at Emery sitting across the table from me while we ate—this was why people took chances.

Life was short. I wasn't going to waste any more of mine worrying if I would be enough for him. I would worry about Dirk, but I would accept his decision. I was going to grab what life was offering. I planned to hold on tight to the man across from me.

Besides, I had always been smart, and I knew we would be stronger together than apart.

Chapter Sixteen

Coast

We pulled up to Kiyaya's place. I'd driven my truck with a trailer attached to haul the windows and roofing supplies we were going to need to do the work on Kiyaya's house. I got out of the driver's side, then moved to the passenger door behind me and helped Mac out.

"Does everyone need to own these monster trucks?" Mac said as I grabbed her around the waist and lifted her out.

It wasn't as hard as I thought it would be to get Mac to agree to come with me. She rescheduled appointments for the days we'd be here, and Dr. Sampson would manage any births or emergencies in her absence.

After the phone call from her brother, she'd had problems sleeping for a few nights. I'd even caught her crying in the bathroom twice. She might have accepted Dirk's choice, but it hadn't kept the hurt his decision caused

175

her. Then she'd worried for days that announcing she loved me after having a freak out, as she called it, would make me question if she really meant it. I told her if it bothered her that much, she could keep telling me over and over until it sank in. Though I knew she loved me because it showed in her eyes every time she looked at me. When she cried, I convinced her she needed time away and asked her to come with me. And it had been the right decision. The more miles away from Shades Valley we'd get—the more she relaxed.

"I'm surprised we didn't get pulled over for Mac not being in a booster seat," Flirt said from the other side of the truck. Both doors were still open, and Mac looked through and flipped him off.

"Mac, you can sit up front on the way home, and I'll sit in the back with Flirt. I don't think I can deal with the two of you bickering on the way home," my dad said as he walked around the front of the truck.

I chuckled and looked at Mac. "Don't listen to either of them. They're just testy because of riding in the cage."

"The trip was only three hours. How can they be bitchy?"

"An hour is too many. Why did the reservation have to put a stop to any alcohol?" my dad griped.

"We hoped it would keep bikers from coming through here, but here you are," Kiyaya said as he stepped out onto the porch.

"Jesus, man, when did you get so old?" my dad teased as he walked toward Kiyaya.

"Eh, have you looked in the mirror lately?" Kiyaya countered, then shook hands with my dad.

As Mac, Flirt, and I walked toward the house, I started introductions, "Kiyaya, this is Flirt. I know you heard me mention him."

"Nice to meet you, Mr. Young," Flirt said and stuck out his hand, and Kiyaya grasped it.

"Eh, you can call me Kiyaya. Mister makes me feel old."

Mac giggled beside me, and I knew she was nervous about meeting my great grandfather.

"Kiyaya, this is Mackenzie. My *áyat*. Mackenzie, my great grandfather, Kiyaya Young."

Kiyaya looked at Mac and tilted his head to the side.

I looked down at Mac and wondered what he saw. She had her auburn hair pulled up in a ponytail, and she wore no make-up, showing the paleness of her skin and freckles across the bridge of her nose. She focused her blue eyes on Kiyaya.

"Back in my great grandfather's time, the Yakima would have stolen you," Kiyaya said.

My lips twitched as I watched Mac stare back at Kiyaya, waiting to hear her response.

"Hmm… if the Yakima warriors and braves looked like your great grandson, I'm not sure I would have put up a fight," Mac answered, and both my dad and Flirt snorted.

Kiyaya chuckled, then looked at me. "If she is your woman, you'd be wise to make her a *ásham, áswan.*"

"Plan to, Kiyaya," I answered, and Kiyaya nodded. I had every intention of making Mac my wife, so there was no reason to deny it.

Kiyaya took Mac and my dad inside while Flirt and I unhitched the trailer. We'd start working on the house the next day.

After we ate dinner with Kiyaya, we sat and talked for a bit before my dad and Flirt left for the motel outside the reservation where they would be staying. Mac and I would stay at Kiyaya's. It would be a tight fit for her and me in the bed, but I wouldn't ever complain about getting to hold her close.

When Kiyaya pulled out the checkers and asked Mac if she wanted to play, she smiled and sat across from him. I watched as they played and wondered if Mac was a sore loser. Instead, at the end of the game, she'd won. At Kiyaya's grunt and the look on his face at losing, I laughed. Kiyaya stood, said goodnight, and went to bed.

The next day, we started on the roof. With Kiyaya's house being on the small side, it only took eight hours to strip the old material off and put the new roof on. When I worked laying the last two sheets of shingles, Flirt climbed down the ladder, and then my dad followed him. I finished and was on my way across the roof when two things happened. Mac screamed, and I watched the top of the ladder slide to the side, then out of view. When I reached where I could see over the edge, my dad laid flat on his back on the ground and Mac was running toward him.

Flirt grabbed the ladder and leaned it back against the house, and I hurried down and to my dad's side. His eyes were closed, and Mac kneeled over him as she reached her hand toward his neck.

"I don't think I need your services, sweetheart. I can promise no baby is on the way," my dad said as he opened his eyes and stared up at Mac. "I'm pretty sure I only knocked the wind out of me."

"Well, I'm still going to check you out, and you won't even have to put your legs up."

"Christ, old man. You scared ten years off me," I said, and he chuckled, then groaned.

"Ten years ain't even close to the years you boys took off me and the other dads with your antics. Now, how about helping me up? I have a feeling I'm going to be a little sore later."

"Not until I make sure you didn't break anything or injure your back," Mac said, not giving my dad a chance to argue. She started at his neck and worked her way down.

"What happened?" Kiyaya asked as he walked out of the house carrying two glasses. "I go inside, and you decide to jump off the roof."

"Hell, I would have been more prepared if I had. I was three-quarters of the way down and lost my footing. Went off balance, and the damn ladder shifted."

"You're not helping tomorrow. Coast and I can get the windows installed by ourselves," Flirt spoke for the first time, and I knew it had scared the brother as much as it had me.

"Any part of your back hurt? Tingling in your legs?" Mac asked, and my dad shook his head no. She asked him more questions, then looked up at me. "Help him sit up. I don't think he broke anything," Mac said, and Flirt and I took a side and, using our hands behind his shoulders, lifted him to a sitting position.

Mac asked about dizziness and nausea. She ran her hands down his spine. "Alright. Let's see how he does on his feet."

Flirt and I each grabbed under an arm and lifted until my dad stood.

"You were lucky, Cruz. And as much as it pains me, I'm going to agree with Flirt. You are benched from helping anymore."

"You can sit with us." Kiyaya waved between him and Mac. "And supervise from the porch, Emilo," Kiyaya said and sat in one chair while he waved his hand at the empty one beside him.

"Damn, we are finished," I said after assessing the last window we installed. It opened and closed with ease.

"Good thing we got them installed this week. The temperature is supposed to drop next week. Kiyaya won't have to burn as much wood either when winter hits," Flirt said and stood back and looked at the front of the house.

"The new roof will help, too," I said and turned when I heard the truck turning in.

"At least we didn't have to work and listen to that trio giving suggestions. It was a clever idea to tell them they should go to the casino for a couple of hours. Perfect timing on our part, too."

"Thanks, brother, I thought so." I patted Flirt's shoulder. "I appreciate the help." Then I set the tool case on the porch. I'd pack it away in the truck later before Flirt and my dad left for the motel.

"Anytime, you know that. We still heading back in the morning?" Flirt asked as Kiyaya, Mac, and my dad got out of the truck.

"Yeah, we can head out as soon as we hitch the trailer once you and my dad get here in the morning."

"Sounds good."

I looked at Mac as she walked toward me. The smile on her face was huge. "I won two hundred and fifty dollars," Mac said when she reached me.

"That's great, *cariño*. Did you win at poker, blackjack, or slots?"

"Oh, she hit on the slots all right. A penny slot machine," my dad griped.

"Don't get all snippy because you played poker and lost."

"Because you kept coming by and asking how I was doing."

"Well, if me coming by made you lose, why didn't you win when I left?"

Kiyaya walked by me and Flirt. "I'm going to lie down. Those two make this old Indian's ears feel like they are bleeding." He opened the door and closed it behind him.

"Was the chase to lock her down worth it?" Flirt asked as my dad and Mac continued to jab at each other.

"Every minute. It's going to sound sappy but being with her is better than I imagined it would be. I fill whole, brother, for the first time in life."

"You deserve it," Flirt said and slapped my back.

I watched and listened, finding humor with my dad and Mac going back and forth. Mac gave as good as she got. And from the crinkling of the skin at the corner of my dad's eyes, he was enjoying their verbal duel.

"Are we sure this truck is going to make it back?" Mac asked as we walked toward Kiyaya's truck.

Flirt and my dad had taken off to the motel. Flirt wanted to clean up, and instead of coming back to have dinner at Kiyaya's, he and my dad said they'd grab something to eat closer to the motel.

While Kiyaya napped, I cleaned up, and then Mac and I drove to the grocery store. I wanted to restock things for Kiyaya before we left tomorrow.

"It will be fine. I checked stuff out and changed the oil when I was here the last time."

"What is he even doing with the truck? He mentioned on the car ride over to the casino that he doesn't drive anymore."

"Yeah, Suni takes him when she has to go."

"Then why not get rid of the truck?"

"He likes having it in case of an emergency," I said as we came to a stoplight. I glanced to my right and looked at the building that sat on the corner with a sign on it that read ICWA.

I turned and pulled into the parking lot. "It won't take long. I want to check on two boys I met the last time I was here. Maybe I can catch the caseworker who was with them."

"Oh, this is like the reservation's own social services," Mac said, and I nodded.

"Yes, they are involved when children from the reservation go into the system. They placed the boys in different homes while the agency waited for a family to have two spots available. Mrs. Stone, the caseworker, said they would do their best to place them together. I wanted to check if that happened," I said and got out on my side, then walked around to help Mac out.

"Why did they go into the system in the first place?" Mac asked as we walked into the building.

"Their mom died from an overdose. No dads around or any other family."

"That's so sad."

"Yeah," I answered, then pointed to the door we needed to go through. "Should be in there if she's in the office today."

When we walked through the door, Mrs. Stone sat at a desk on the phone, and sitting in chairs off to the side were the boys I had come to check on. Their heads bent as they focused on their laps.

As we walked toward Mrs. Stone, she raised her head, and I saw recognition in her eyes. She held up her finger, and Mac and I waited while she finished her conversation.

"Yes, I'll have them there within the hour," she said to whomever was on the other side of the call. She hung up and then looked at us. "Mr. Cortez, right?"

"Emery. And this is Mackenzie Minton."

Mrs. Stone looked over at Tracker and Paxton as she stood and walked around her desk. "I'll be back in a minute. You boys stay here."

When neither boy acknowledged her, Mrs. Stone sighed, but didn't say anything else to the boys. "We can talk over there." She pointed and walked across the room, putting as much distance between the boys and us as the large room allowed.

"What's going on, Mrs. Stone?" I asked.

Mrs. Stone sighed, then took a deep breath and blew it out. "Tracker ran from the foster home I placed him in. He heard the parents talking about how long it was going to be before Tracker and Paxton were placed together. He'd also heard them mention Paxton's foster parents' name. He won't say how he found out where they lived, but he did, and he took off. I'm assuming the couple of times the two foster mothers met to allow the boys to spend time together, he found out where their home was located. Then he ran from his foster parents' home and found Paxton's foster family's home. When Paxton was outside playing, he approached Paxton, and they took off together. They were located after a couple of hours, and the reason they are here.

"I found a temporary home. It's a foster family whose kids are with their birth mom right now on visitation. The boys will stay be able to stay for two weeks, giving us time to find another available place for them."

"You said that is why they are here. So this just happened today?" I asked, clarifying what she was telling us.

"I mentioned to you before, we do our best. It may not look like it sometimes, but we do work with the children's best interest in mind."

"Not in those two boys' case. They're eight damn weeks in the system and going to a second home, and in two weeks, they will be moved to a third home. I don't know how you can say you are looking out for the children's best interest with a straight face."

Mac placed a hand on my forearm. "Emery."

I took a deep breath. "I'm sorry, Mrs. Stone. I get you can only work with what you have. Why aren't they going back to the foster homes they were in before?"

"The foster for Tracker didn't want to have him placed back with them because he ran, and they have four other foster children in their home to worry about. Paxton's family feels the same about placing Paxton back into their home, but their reason is Tracker knows where they live. And they don't want to worry that Tracker will show up again to take Paxton away."

"So the boys are going to the temporary home today?"

"Yes."

"Would you mind if I spoke to them for a few minutes?"

She nodded. "I'll run to the restroom and fax a few things while you're talking to them.

"Can I ask a few questions before you go?" Mac asked Mrs. Stone.

"Sure."

"Is there anything more a foster parent has to do when the tribal agency is involved?"

"We follow the state guidelines. The difference is this office has a say over children from the reservation, even though they can be placed outside of its lands. When a Native American child is fostered, or even adopted, we request the parents encourage the history and traditions related to the child's heritage be kept up with. Involvement with the tribe, if they live close enough, is encouraged. Otherwise, teaching them about their culture."

"Thank you, Mrs. Stone," Mac answered.

"I'll be back momentarily." Mrs. Stone turned and walked across the room and out the door.

"Why did you want to know all that?"

"Curious," she answered. But somehow, I knew there was more going on in her head.

Chapter Seventeen

Mac

As we approached the two boys, they lifted their heads and looked up at us. What I saw in their eyes broke my heart.

"Hi," I said and smiled. The younger one smiled back, but it didn't reach his eyes.

"You're the man from the clinic," the older boy said as he looked at Emery.

"Yes. I heard you've been having a rough time of it."

He shrugged. "They separated us. I couldn't do what you told me. I can't protect him if I not there."

"Sometimes, you lead by example. Mrs. Stone's working on getting you placed together. It's just taking a little time. Why'd you run, Tracker?" Emery asked, and I knew from the boy's expression he didn't want to answer.

"Because of me," the young boy said.

"Pax," Tracker said as a warning, but I watched as Paxton looked at his brother, then to Emery, who had taken the empty chair beside him.

"I got to see Tracker a couple of times, and I cried because I missed him. So, to get me to stop, he told me he would find a way for us to get back together. And he did, but they found us. Now we have no place to go 'cause the other families don't want us back."

I turned my head and discreetly as I could, wiped the corners of my eyes.

"Who are you?" Tracker asked me.

"Mackenzie. It's nice to meet you, Tracker."

"There's nothing nice about me," he said, and I found it strange how he said it.

"Did someone tell you that?" I asked.

"Does it matter? Not like you can do anything about it."

"Hey, you don't get to talk to her that way," Emery scolded.

I touched his shoulder. "It's okay."

"No, it's not," he said to me, then turned back to Tracker. "You don't ever disrespect a woman, and you definitely don't disrespect *my* woman. Anger isn't going to get you anywhere. Other than in a heap of trouble. You are going to come across many people in your life, Tracker. Some won't have a problem with you. But others won't like the color of your skin, how you talk, how you dress, where you come from. Their opinions of you don't matter unless you make it matter. Respect yourself, accept who you are, where you come from—let the other people show their ignorance, and don't let their ignorance reflect on you."

Tracker looked at me. "Sorry."

"It takes a big man to realize when he's wrong," I said.

"I'm twelve."

I smiled at Tracker. "Well, that is why you realized it was wrong."

"I'm seven," Paxton piped up.

I smiled at him, too. "I bet you know when you're wrong, too. Huh?"

"Yep. You're pretty," he said, and Emery nudged his shoulder.

"You trying to hit on my woman?" Emery asked, and Paxton grinned.

I touched Emery's shoulder and waited for him to look at me. "I'll be right back. I'm going to run to the restroom."

"Okay, these guys will keep me entertained," he said and winked at the boys.

I walked out of the door and looked up and down the hallway. When I spotted Mrs. Stone talking with a man, I walked toward her. As I approached, she turned and then excused herself from their conversation to address me.

"I tried to give Mr. Cortez a little extra time with the boys. Are the two of you ready to leave?"

"Emery's talking with them. I came to find you."

"Oh."

"Yes. Mrs. Stone, I've passed the state's requirements to be a foster parent, but I've never actively taken any kids since they approved me. Would you be able to check with the state and see if my original acceptance is still valid? It has been a while, but all my information is the same. When they approved me, I held off because I was getting my practice up and running. They understood and said I only needed to call when I was ready to accept foster children into my home. I think I might be ready."

Mrs. Stone smiled. "If you'll walk back to the office with me, I'll look that information up now."

"I'd rather call you in a couple of days. Would there be an issue if I wanted to foster Tracker and Paxton? You said the ICWA likes for the children to have access to the tribe, so the children don't lose the knowledge of their culture because of circumstances that separate them from the tribe."

"Yes. But depending on where you live, we understand not all fosters or even adoptive parents of Native American children are going to live close to the reservation a child originated from. There are other ways for parents to show and instruct a child about where they come from and their background and history of their people."

"I understand the reasoning for that, Mrs. Stone. In any mixed-race family, no one should have to give up their ethnicity to fit into someone else's."

"When I spoke with Mr. Cortez before, he said he was single. Has that changed, or will it be changing, perhaps?"

"Maybe, but he doesn't know it yet. He doesn't even know I'm speaking with you."

Mrs. Stone chuckled, then looked me in the eye, her expression back to serious. "If everything is in order with your license, putting two Native American children in your care, it would definitely improve your chances if you were married to a Native American. Marriage isn't required per the state's qualifications to become a foster. You could take it on as a single foster parent."

"Do you think the state would place them with us? I knew I didn't have to be married, but they've had a single mom and it didn't work out for them. I want to show them the other side. The side where a dad sticks around to take care of them. Not because it is an obligation, but because he wants to be there. The side where two parents are committed to take care of and protect them."

"Mr. Cortez talked with the boys when they first came into foster care. He showed patience. He gave sound advice. He strikes me as the type of man who would be strict but fair. Two boys with Tracker and Paxton's history will need someone like that at some point if they are to succeed. Plus, I know he has family here on the reservation, so the boys will not lose out on any opportunity to keep up with their culture if placed in your home. We will have to do an in-house inspection update since you haven't had any children in your home yet.

"If all goes well, I'll support you both and help in any way I can. My gut tells me Mr. Cortez may be exactly who those two boys need. I tend to follow my gut; it has done well for me over the years. I'll be waiting for your call, Ms. Minton."

"Actually, it's Doctor Minton," I informed her.

"Then I'll be waiting for your call, Doctor Minton."

"Thank you for taking the time to talk with me."

"Do you mind me asking what type of doctor you are?"

"Not at all. It isn't a secret and not as if you won't find out when you check my application out. I'm an OBGYN. I specialize in high-risk pregnancies."

The smile on Mrs. Stone's face broadened. "This just keeps getting better. I really hope you're serious about your inquiry, Dr. Minton."

"I am. And thank you again, Mrs. Stone. I better get back before Emery wonders what's taking me so long."

Mrs. Stone fell in step with me. "Can I ask why? Why Tracker and Paxton?"

"Well, when we walked into the room and I saw their heads bent and their posture. It was the sign of defeat and acceptance in what life dealt them. And I didn't even know who they were or what they had been through. Then I saw their eyes, and they reflected the same. But as they talked, I realized they haven't lost all their spark. As I watched Emery with them, and how they responded to him. How could I not want to intervene? If I can give them a home and a better life, why shouldn't I? I'm unable to have children, Mrs. Stone, so I look at Tracker and Paxton and not only can I help them—I think they'll help me."

Mrs. Stone nodded in understanding, then we walked back toward her office.

"Got something on your mind, *cariño?*" Emery asked as we walked into his house.

After talking with Tracker and Paxton, and Mrs. Stone, we'd driven back to Kiyaya's place. I knew I'd been subdued at dinner, even the next day on the drive back to Shades Valley. I caught Emery glancing at me several times in the truck, and even Flirt and Cruz looked at me oddly.

I was excited and nervous. And I wondered if I'd made a rash decision while talking with the boys and watching Emery with them. Now, I needed to either step back or trust my gut as Mrs. Stone did.

I felt Emery's eyes on me as we stood in the living room and he waited for me to acknowledge his question.

Instead, I took a deep breath and asked a question of my own. "Would you marry me?"

The stunned look on his face had me rethinking everything. How could I parent two boys if I couldn't even handle my issues without second-guessing myself at every turn? And my God, we had barely closed the door to his house and I'm blurting out crazy shit.

I turned toward the stairway, intending to go shower and crawl into bed and forget everything. Hopefully, I hadn't ruined what we were building between us. But why would a man want to put up with my crazy?

"Oh no, you don't drop something like that and run away," he said. When I turned back to face him, he was right there, looking down at me. "Do I not rate the whole deal? You know, down on one knee and the proclamation of your undying love before you pop the question? Do you have a ring for me?"

"If you are going to make fun of me, then forget I asked."

"I don't think so. If you recall, you caught the bouquet, and I caught the garter. Who are we to thumb our noses at tradition?"

"Do you want me on my knees?" I asked, and when his lips quirked up, I realized what I'd said.

"Oh, I definitely want you on your knees, but later. I love you, Mac. Spending the rest of my life with you makes saying yes, the easiest thing I have done in my life. But what brought this on?"

I took a deep breath, then spilled about my talk with Mrs. Stone about fostering the boys. He stood silent when I finished, and I worried I might have read him wrong regarding his interest in what happened to them.

"Jesus, I'm not sure what I've done in my life to deserve you, but I'm not questioning it now. Yes, *cariño*, I'll marry you." He held his arms open, and I walked into them and laid my head on his chest.

"Since you're being so cooperative, can we do it as soon as the three day waiting period is up on the license?"

"Are you in a hurry to make an honest man out of me?"

I pinched his nipple through his t-shirt. "No, but I'd like Tracker and Paxton to have an actual home before their time is up at the temporary foster placement. Or at least before the holidays. Though I think the perfect home for them would be with us."

"You never cease to amaze me. I need to tell you, when I first met the boys, Mrs. Stone told me I should apply to be a foster parent. If I'd thought the state would have approved my application, I might have worked on getting one. Something about those boys got to me."

"I will always give *you* what you need, Emery," giving back to him the words he'd given to me on more than one occasion. "Those boys need a home, a real one. And watching you interact with them, did it for me. I think the boys were what I was waiting for."

"You have it wrong, *cariño*. You were meant for me, Tracker, and Paxton. We were only waiting for you to find us," he said, then lifted me in his arms and carried me up the stairs.

Four days later, standing in front of the judge at the courthouse, Emery and I exchanged vows in front of our friends. Afterward, we celebrated and watched those same friends hand over money to Cruz.

Flirt tried to argue that Cruz had an unfair advantage. But Emery's dad argued that as Emery's best friends, they should have spent less time watching him, and more time watching me. That if they paid any attention to how I looked at his son, they would have known. They'd all groaned when he added, "Besides, no woman can resist us Cortez men." Then he turned and winked at me as he stuffed the cash in his pocket.

Unknowingly, I had been his ace in the hole. I also wasn't going to dispute the comment on resisting the Cortez men. River had been right—the dads were just as hard to resist as their sons.

Chapter Eighteen

Coast

"Jesus, *mi esposa*, you're going to bounce out of your seat." Christ, I would never grow tired of calling her my wife. Mac nervously tried to stay still in her seat. Tracker and Paxton would be lucky if she didn't latch on to them and not let go until they were old enough to leave home to be on their own.

It had taken two weeks to get the all-clear on fostering the two boys. They hadn't been told who was fostering them, only that they had a family with room for two. It had worked out perfectly. They'd been at the temporary foster home expecting to be moved into two separate places again until Mrs. Stone had visited them and told them there had been a change, and they would be going to the same home.

My house had gone from just me to Mac moving in after we'd married. Now it would house two more. Their rooms were ready and filled with things to reflect their ages.

197

Per my wife, because I'd thought it would be more efficient to buy two of everything in the furniture store and call it a day.

"I can't help it. Things have gone so smoothly, I keep waiting for something to come along and ruin it," Mac said and looked toward the door for what had to be the hundredth time.

I placed my arm around her shoulder and pulled her into me. "You're going to be a great mom."

"Hah, see how much you know. I'm going to be a neurotic mess, and you are going to have to keep it together, so the boys don't run scared."

"Anything for you."

The door opened and Mrs. Stone walked in with Tracker and Paxton carrying a trash bag with their stuff. It wasn't even a large trash bag.

"Oh, Emery."

"I see it. Those bags will be a distant memory by nightfall."

Mrs. Stone walked past us and winked.

I looked toward the boys. "Hey, how's it going?"

"We're being moved again. At least this time we'll be together, and I hope we can stay until we're old enough to be on our own," Paxton said and looked around the empty room.

"They're not here yet, Pax," Tracker said and sat down, dropping his bag on the floor at his side. Paxton followed his older brother and did the same.

"What are you doing here?" Tracker asked.

"Waiting to pick up two boys," Mac said, and I wanted to laugh because if not for my hand on her thigh, I was sure she would have catapulted out of her seat.

"They're not here either. Bet you'll be cool foster parents," Paxton said and sighed.

"Ya think so, huh?" Mac grinned.

"Uh huh, 'cause you talked to us and you didn't even have to."

Mrs. Stone walked to the printer in the corner and pulled off the sheets that had come through. She flipped through them, then looked at us and nodded. She had the official paperwork in hand. We were ready.

"Hey, since the family isn't here to pick you up, and the boys aren't here for us to take home. I say we just go together," I said and watched Paxton and Tracker actually think about it. God, the two of them were going to be a handful.

"I don't think they'd let you do that," Tracker said and sighed.

Paxton chewed his lip, then looked at Mac. "We could leave when Mrs. Stone isn't looking. Maybe they wouldn't find us this time," Paxton said and looked to Tracker for his okay.

Holy hell, I would have to watch the two. At least until they felt comfortable in our home.

"I'm ready, Mr. and Mrs. Cortez. I just need your signature on these copies," Mrs. Stone said and turned the paperwork around on her desk and set a pen on top.

Mac and I stood and walked to the desk. Mac signed, and then I did. We were officially the foster parents contracted to Tracker and Paxton.

"If you're coming with us, let's hit the road. We have a three hours' drive to get to the house," I said and looked at both boys.

"I baked cookies yesterday for you. And when we get to the house, you'll meet our friends. There are even a few kids and several more on the way. Everyone's waiting to meet you guys," Mac rambled nervously.

It had taken a second for the two boys to figure out what was going on. Tracker was the first to catch on.

"For real? We are staying with the two of you?" Tracker stood.

"Yes, you are. Mr. and Mrs. Cortez are officially your new foster parents. I'll come once a month for a home visit," she said to the boys, then turned to Mac and me. "I'll let you know ahead of time, so you both have ample time to be off." She then turned back to the boys. "It took some time, but I did my best to get you placed together. Congratulations, boys. Because I think you're going to enjoy this home and find it had been worth a little inconvenience."

I was proud of Mac. She held back as long as she could. "Can I have a hug, Paxton? I'm so happy we get to be a part of you grow up."

Paxton latched on to Mac when she opened her arms. He cried along with her. When I looked over at Tracker, he stood watching, his expression one of longing, but he stayed in place.

"Hope you're ready, bud. She's gonna want to hug you, too."

Tracked sighed, "I guess I could let her if she needs to."

Mac released Paxton and turned to Tracker expectantly. "You might as well get used to it. I'm going to do it a lot, so fair warning."

Tracker stared at her and slowly stepped forward. When he finally was close enough, Mac stepped in and closed the distance. She wrapped her arms around him until he moved his arms and hugged her back.

"You've done a good thing. Both of you are going to be good for them," Mrs. Stone said in a low voice beside me.

"It's Mac. She's going to be the best thing that has happened for the three of us," I said as I watched Tracker. He and Mac broke apart, then Tracker turned his head and wiped his eyes.

Mrs. Stone smiled. "Funny, on the phone the other day, Mac said the same about you."

The first part of the drive back to Shades Valley was quiet. Tracker and Paxton had never been off the reservation, so they'd spent the time with their noses smashed to the windows, taking in everything around them.

We stopped and ate, and when we sat and it came time to order, the two boys looked at one another.

"Get whatever you want," I said and was glad to see them relax. It made me wonder what went on in the other foster homes or with their mother. It didn't really matter to me because they'd never have to worry about having enough to eat. Or even where they were going to sleep from one week to the next.

The way Mac had already taken the boys under her wing, I knew we'd have the adoption talk soon. And I was good with it. It was odd because they already felt like mine.

We pulled off the main road and reached the gate at the compound. I let the window down and gave the prospect a chin lift and drove through.

"That's where we're going to live?" Paxton asked and pointed.

I chuckled. "No, that's the clubhouse. It's used for meetings, gatherings, things like that."

"Oh."

"All this land belongs to your motorcycle club?" Tracker asked.

"Yes."

"Cool. Are Paxton and I sharing a room?"

"No, you each have your own room with a shared bathroom between them," Mac answered.

Through the rearview mirror, I saw Tracker smile. It was the first real one he'd had all day. Being the oldest, no doubt he'd take the longest to adjust. Paxton would embrace the changes easier.

Following the road to where I lived, I shook my head when the homes came into view.

Everyone was outside, and there were balloons attached to my porch railing along with a banner that read 'Welcome to the Black Hawk MC Tracker and Paxton.'

"What's the big garage for at that house?" Tracker asked as passed by Speed's.

"That's where my brothers and I build custom bikes."

"Will you teach me?" His question surprised me.

"You want to learn how to build bikes, Tracker?"

"It'd be cool."

"Then I'll teach you."

"Can I learn, too?" Paxton asked.

"Sure thing, Pax."

"Are all those people part of your club?" Tracker stared out the window at the group.

"Sure are. And it's your club now, too, Tracker."

He didn't respond, and I noticed he went quiet when he was either upset or didn't want to share what he thought. Mac and I would work on getting him to trust enough that he felt comfortable telling us anything.

I pulled the truck on the side of the house, and everyone got out. Paxton walked beside Mac and held her hand. Tracker walked boldly out in front of us. The kid had a backbone for sure, and I was glad to see it.

We reached the front of the house where my brothers with their ol' ladies and kids stood with huge smiles.

I introduced the boys, then Mac took over with introducing the adults to Tracker and Paxton. It wouldn't take long for the boys to remember everyone.

The kids' introductions were saved for last, and I noticed Ally, Neely, Paxton, and Tracker were having a stare-off. Sami noticed it, too, and nudged Ally's shoulder.

Ally sighed loudly and stepped closer to the boys. "Hi, I'm Ally. Welcome to Black Hawk," she said with no enthusiasm in her voice.

"Why don't you try that again?" Sami scolded.

"Fine. But can someone around here please have a girl? We're drowning in penises."

Tracker and Paxton burst out laughing. Which was the first sign things would work out, eventually.

Chapter Nineteen

Mac

I walked into the bedroom and pushed the door until I heard the click. When I turned back, Emery sat on the bed, leaning against the headboard with a smile on his face.

"You know you don't have to check on them every hour, right?"

I stuck my tongue out at him, and he chuckled. "For your information, I was making sure they were asleep. We still need to set things out from Santa for Paxton. And don't forget to eat the cookies and make it look like you drank the milk. Paxton set the plate and glass on the table by the tree."

"I was there when he did it, *cariño*."

"That's right. I just don't want to forget anything," I said and sat down on the end of the bed.

Emery patted the bed beside him. "Come here."

I crawled up the bed and rested back against the headboard like Emery.

"Rest for a minute. You've been going for days. From baking cookies to wrapping the presents, and the food you've been cooking. We'll never eat all of it. Did I mention the ham and turkey you baked were excellent? And the stuffing, and the mashed potatoes, and the green bean casserole…"

"Stop it." I chuckled and smacked his stomach. "The entire club was at the clubhouse. We needed the food. Did you not see the three turkeys after everyone got finished eating? Luna picked what meat they left on the bones for Karma, and there wasn't much. Two hams were demolished, and the desserts Claire brought. I almost lost a hand reaching for the last strawberry cheesecake cupcake."

Emery lifted my hand to his mouth and kissed it. "Who dared to deprive you of a cupcake?"

"Kiyaya!"

Cruz had driven to the reservation the day before and picked up Kiyaya and drove back to Black Hawk without Emery or I knowing about it. When Emery answered the door after someone knocked, the surprise at seeing Kiyaya was priceless. I didn't understand until Cruz explained Kiyaya had never visited Black Hawk, even though through the years he'd been invited.

The bed shook as Emery laughed. He grabbed his stomach and groaned. "Shit, I'm full. Stop hitting me and making me laugh."

"Serves you right. It isn't funny. We both reached for it, but I grabbed it first. I was raising it to my mouth when he

206

commented, *I don't need all that sugar, anyway. Even though this could be my last Christmas'.*"

"Ahh, *cariño*, I'm sorry you didn't get your cupcake."

"What are you talking about? I didn't give it to him. I told him we'd miss him next year and ate it in front of him."

Emery pulled me closer, and I rested my head on his shoulder. He kissed the top of my head, then leaned his head against mine.

"I believe they are getting comfortable here. They weren't as quiet around the brothers at dinner," Emery said. He worried more than I did about Tracker and Paxton.

"It's going to take them a while, honey. They've been here less than three months. And as far as being quiet around your brothers, have you tried getting some of them to talk? Then there's Roscoe. That man could carry on a conversation by himself. I saw Sue walk by and pop him on the shoulder four or five times for saying inappropriate stuff. It might be a good idea to keep Kiyaya away from him while he is here," I said and sighed, then wiggled my toes.

Christmas Eve dinner with the entire club and their families had been loud and fun. And I'd never seen a group of men put away so much food. Anything left, we made individual dinner packages and sent them home with the single men. All the women in the club fixed the food, which had been planned out weeks ago. The only woman who'd gotten out of cooking was Carly. She brought the paper products and drinks because Crusher had told us ahead of time that unless we wanted half the club in the ER, then we needed to avoid assigning her any food dishes.

Christmas Day, the men would spend with their families. The ones with no family would spend the day with Sue and Roscoe this year. Black Hawk made sure none of their members spent the holiday alone.

"I might have gone overboard with presents," I said, and Emery snorted.

"You hit overboard a couple of weeks ago. I'm not sure what you would call the boxes and shit in our closet."

"I want them to have the best Christmas since they've never really had one."

"We can't erase everything they've been through. But we can change their future. They'll never have to worry about having food, clean clothes, or a bed to sleep in ever again. And it will take time for them to adjust to having those things every day without worrying if the next day it is all going to vanish. One day at a time, Mac."

"I know."

"I think it's safe for us to tote the stuff downstairs and put it under the tree," Emery said, and I nodded.

"We better get started because if I don't get up now, I'm going to fall asleep." I yawned.

After what felt like a hundred trips up and down the stairs, I stood with Emery in front of the Christmas tree.

"Our first Christmas," I said as I watched the lights on the tree fade, then come back in assorted colors.

"There is one thing missing from the tree," Emery said and bent down, picking up a package. When he stood back up, he handed it to me. "Open it. It's for the tree."

I tore the paper off to find a white box with a lid. I lifted the top and inside, surrounded in material to keep it from breaking, was a crystal ornament. It was round with etched snowflakes. The globe was beautiful, but the words on it were what made my eyes fill with moisture.

2019
First Christmas
Family
It's what you make of it.

"It's beautiful, Emery. Here, you put it on the tree." I held the box while Emery lifted the ornament, then positioned it front and center on the tree.

"Love you, *cariño*."

"Love you, more."

We watched the lights reflect on the crystal ornament and absorbed the moment before we headed upstairs.

Tomorrow would be anything but peaceful.

I opened my eyes to darkness, then lifted my head from Emery's chest and glanced over at the clock. It read two forty-five in the morning. I laid my head back down on his chest and shut my eyes and concentrated on his heartbeat.

It hadn't helped. I was too excited about Christmas. Not so much for me, but for Tracker and Paxton. I couldn't wait to see their faces.

Last Christmas, I spent it alone. Dirk had been in Afghanistan, and he and I had no other family. My eyes filled thinking of my brother dealing with everything alone. It still stung that he hadn't wanted me in Maryland. I'd honored his wish and stayed away. I even understood, to a point, that he needed to do things on his own. I'd given him his time, and when he'd told me he was being fitted for his prosthetic, I'd invited him to come for Christmas. I wanted him to meet Emery and the boys, but he'd made excuses and said he'd make the trip in the spring.

"What's the matter, *mi esposa*?"

"I woke up and now I can't go back to sleep," I said and snuggled closer.

"Who would have thought you'd be more excited about Christmas morning than Tracker and Paxton?"

"I can't help it. I'm so happy, then I feel guilty for being so happy because Dirk is alone when he doesn't have to be. And before you say it, I know it isn't about me. But it has only been the two of us for a while. From the time we lost our parents, we've only spent a handful of the holidays together. Dirk was either deployed or I was working. I don't want him to be the uncle the boys see once every other year if we're lucky."

"Give him time, Mac. He's gotten his prosthetic, and he has therapy. He's essentially learning to walk again. By spring, he should be mobile enough to maneuver around an airport."

"People fly all the time with disabilities. The airlines have agents to help them."

210

"Yes, they do. But you are talking about your brother, the master sergeant who is used to helping others, not having help extended to him."

"You're right."

"Excuse me. Could you repeat that?"

"Stop it. You heard me. I have no problem admitting when you're right. You'd hear it more if you were right more," I said and then was on my back with Emery looming over me.

"I'm right a lot. Like now, for instance."

"How are you right now?"

"Because I know what will help you sleep," he said and bent his head and captured my mouth. As he moved to my neck, I placed my hands on his back, touching him. It was still hard to believe he was mine.

I slid my hands easily down his back. My destination was his butt checks, but my arms fell short.

"Ugh, your body is too long."

I felt the sting from his bite on the tender skin between my neck and shoulder. "It could be you're too short."

"No, I'm pretty sure it is you," I said and felt the vibration from his laughing.

"This will help," he said and flipped us, putting me on top of him.

I pushed until I straddled him and placed my hands on his chest, feeling the muscles and hardness of his body. Once I started, I couldn't stop touching him. He was mine. I traced his nipples with my fingers and teased them, finding it sexy as they grew hard under my touch. I loved time like this with him. Heck, I just loved him. Sometimes my need for him was so much, I would swear I felt fire working its way through my veins.

Leaning forward, I placed my lips on his, and with my tongue, licked across the seam. He parted his lips, and I inserted my tongue. Our tongues met and our tastes melded together.

I broke the kiss and looked down at him, barely making out his eyes in the dark. His heart raced under my hand.

"I'm the luckiest woman."

"Ah, *mi hermosa esposa* (my beautiful wife), I am the lucky one to have caught you."

He grazed my breasts with his fingertips, then rose, bringing himself to a sitting position with me still straddling him. His hard length pressed against the thin material of my panties.

Emery grabbed the hem of my nightshirt and pulled it over my head, tossing it to the side. I rocked my hips, and he groaned.

I gasped when he grabbed hold of my panties and pulled. The lace giving away easily.

He moved his hands and palmed my breasts, and I leaned my head back and enjoyed the roughness of his large hands. He rubbed his palms over the nipples, and they puckered and strained toward him. When he bent and sucked the tip, then bit down gently, I moaned as a shiver ran through my body.

I groaned and ran my hands over his shoulders and down his back and up again until I reached the back of his head. Holding him in place, Emery put all his focus on my breasts. My nipples were hard and tingling as he took turns with each, rolling the nipples and circling his tongue around them.

His hand moved between us, then he cupped my mound, easily finding my clit and brushing a finger across it. I arched my back and pushed my breast further into his mouth. I felt wanton and self-confident in a way I had never felt before with my body until I was with Emery. Being with Emery was amazing, and I got to spend my life with him.

He released my nipple with a little pop and then kissed his way back up my neck and took my mouth, branding me with his kiss.

My core ached, and I rolled my hips. The finger on my nub moved back and forth, then circled, sending me over. As my body rode the orgasm out, he lifted me and brought me down on his cock, filling me.

Emery lifted me up and down over and over until we were both on the brink. With one last push in, his cock pulsed, and we went over the edge the edge together.

He rested his face in the crook of my neck as we both fought to regain our breath. He lifted his head and lifted my body from his. With some maneuvering, he laid us both back on the bed.

I laid my head on his arm, and he pulled me to him and kissed my head.

"That was just what I needed to go back to sleep," I said with a yawn and closed my eyes.

"You're *mi mujer* (my woman), I'll always give you what you need," was the last thing I heard before sleep claimed me.

Chapter Twenty

Coast

"Tracker! Get up! He came! He came!" Paxton yelled. I smiled before I even opened my eyes.

Mac shifted beside me, then buried her head back in her pillow and groaned. "Oh my God, I feel like I just fell asleep. What time is it?"

I glanced over at the clock, then raised my hand to my face and swiped down. It was going to be a long day. "It's five-forty."

I laid there and wondered how long it would be before there was a knock at the bedroom door. I opened my mouth to suggest we better get some clothes on when Mac literally jumped out of the bed.

"Get up. I don't want to miss anything with the boys," she said. After she grabbed clothes, she darted into the bathroom. I shook my head, threw back the covers, and sat up on the side of the bed. I heard the shower running in the

215

bathroom, and I reached for my cell and texted my dad to let him know everyone was up. He texted back, and I grinned. He was bringing Mac's surprise present with him. When I set the phone back down, the expected rap on the bedroom door had me rising.

"Hold on a sec," I yelled and walked to the chair and grabbed my jeans. A woman in the house definitely changed things because before when I'd strip for bed, the clothes would be in a pile on the floor.

Once my jeans were on, I walked to the door and pulled it open to find Tracker and Paxton both in the hall, standing side by side.

"What's got you up so early?" I asked, feigning as if I'd forgotten what day it was. The wide-eyed expression on Paxton's face almost made me laugh.

"It's Christmas," he answered, and the way he said it reminded me of Mac and her excitement from the night before.

"Yes, it is!" Mac said as she walked out of the bathroom dressed and toweling her hair. She must have broken the world record on shower time. She tossed the towel in the hamper, which was another added item to our bedroom, and brushed her hair with her fingers.

"Santa came like you said he would, Mac. I didn't think he would, but he did. I didn't touch anything because there's a lot, and I didn't know if it was mine," Paxton said, barely able to contain himself as he rocked on his heels.

At Paxton's *a lot*, I looked at Mac and lifted a brow. A lot was an understatement. For the last month and a half, every time she came home from work, she had a bag that she'd stash in our closet.

Mac waved me off and walked to Paxton and kneeled in front of him. "Santa doesn't make mistakes often, so whatever is under the tree is for you and Tracker."

Tracker snorted, and I nudged him. He didn't believe in Santa, which was normal for a twelve-year-old, but not for the five-year-old he had been when his mother told him there wasn't a Santa Claus. All because Tracker had cried when he hadn't gotten anything on Christmas morning. I'd never hit a woman, but if that drugged up bitch was still alive, I'd make an exception.

"Mommy said I was naughty, and that's why Santa never brought me anything," Pax said, and I gritted my teeth. Fuck yeah, I would slap that bitch if she was living.

"Mom lied, Pax. The elves probably forgot to add your name to Santa's list," Tracker said.

I placed my hand on Tracker's shoulder and squeezed. One of the first things Mac and I noticed when the boys started living with us was how Tracker always looked out for Pax.

"Do you think so?" Pax looked at me and asked with hopeful eyes. Eyes that had seen way too much for their seven years.

"I'm with your brother. Those elves are busy, and I bet they lose names all the time. It's the only explanation, since you are far from naughty, Pax."

"Well, I say we forget about the elves' past mistakes and go down and check out what Santa brought this year," Mac stood and said. "What do you think, Paxton?"

"Yes!" he yelled and jumped up and down.

"Let me grab a shirt," I said and walked to the dresser and pulled out a t-shirt. I'd take a shower after everything was opened because I figured if I mentioned it then, there would be mutiny.

"What is all the racket? An old man can't get any sleep around here," Kiyaya said as he shuffled out of the extra bedroom.

"Santa came!" Paxton informed him, as if everyone in the house hadn't heard him earlier.

"Eh, you don't say." Kiyaya smiled down at Paxton, then glanced over at me. "Are we going to stand here or go downstairs and let the boy inspect his bounty?"

"We're going. Not like the man in red left your old ass anything." Mac smacked my arm, and I chuckled.

"Can you even remember the last time you got something from Santa, Kiyaya?" Tracker said, then looked at me and smiled. I winked at him and grinned. It was good to see Tracker was becoming comfortable enough to joke. I couldn't wait for the day he and Paxton lost the unsure looks I would catch sometimes in their eyes.

"Stop ganging up on Kiyaya. Are you going to call your dad and let him know we are up? He mentioned that yesterday after the club dinner. He wanted to come watch the boys open their gifts."

"Yeah, I already did while you were showering. I didn't think Paxton and Tracker would want to wait. Or you, either."

"Whatever. I'm just excited for the boys. So, let's get moving," she said and walked out of the bedroom with Paxton and Tracker on her heels.

Kiyaya snickered. "Eh, you might have bitten off more than you can chew with that girl. She's not going to let you boys get by with much."

"I kind of like how she handles you, Kiyaya. How was that cupcake?" I asked as we started down the stairs. My lips twitched when Kiyaya began mumbling.

"Look, Emery, I got books, cars, games, and a PlayStation! Santa even brought a Xbox for Tracker!" Paxton announced as Kiyaya and I walked into the living room. Pax sat on the floor in front of the tree, inspecting everything piled in front of him.

I looked over at Tracker, who had his head down as he looked at the gaming system box and the games we'd gotten for it. Or that Santa had dropped off.

"Hey, bud, after pops gets here and we open gifts. I'll help you get that set up."

"Okay," Tracker answered, his voice a little rough, and I frowned. When Mac touched my arm, I looked down at her, and she shook her head slightly. I mouthed what, and she nodded toward the kitchen.

"Kiyaya, you want coffee? It should be done. I hit the switch when I got downstairs. Or would you rather have tea?" she asked over her shoulder as I walked with her to the kitchen.

"Coffee sounds good, Mackenzie," Kiyaya answered.

Once we were out of earshot, I asked again, "What?"

Mac turned, and it shocked me to see the moisture in her eyes. "Tracker needed a minute. Oh, Emery. His face when Paxton told him the Xbox had his name on it. We know he doesn't believe in Santa and goes along with it because of Paxton. Hell, I wanted to cry when he bent and picked up that box, then looked over his shoulder at me and mouthed thank you. I mean, he's twelve, Emery, and it breaks my heart he's had to spend his childhood looking after Paxton when he should have been enjoying his own." I watched Mac's transformation from being on the brink of tears to a pissed off woman. "If that woman… and I use the word loosely because I'm trying to be polite… were alive, I'd shake the shit out of her." Mac turned away and began pouring coffee into cups.

"*Cariño.*"

"I know, I know. I can't let the stuff get to me. We can only make going forward better for them. Good God, Emery, he barely could answer you for being choked up. That's why I brought you in here. He needed a moment to compose himself."

"And maybe you did, too," I said and ran my hand from the top of her head down until I reached her back and stopped to rub it.

"Yes, and now, I'm good. We will spend the rest of the morning and day enjoying and being thankful for what we have," Mac said while she placed the coffee cups on a tray.

When she finished, I picked the tray up, and we walked into the living room. Tracker was better and sat on the floor by the coffee table, with Paxton at his side. Kiyaya was on the other side of the coffee table, sitting on the couch. I smiled when I saw what was on the table between them. A checkerboard.

I went to set the tray down when there was a knock on the front door.

"Why is your dad knocking? He knows we're expecting him," Mac said, and I shrugged.

"I do not know. Let him in, and you can ask him," I answered and put the tray down as she started toward the front door.

Mac opened the door, and I barely heard her whispered, "Oh my God."

The boys and Kiyaya turned toward the door to see what was going on.

"Merry Christmas, sis." Mac's brother, Dirk, said as he stood on crutches in the open doorway. He'd barely gotten the words out before Mac lunged and wrapped her arms around him. Luckily, my dad had been behind Dirk to give him support from the onslaught, or it would have ended with Dirk being taken to the ground with Mac on top of him.

"You going to let your brother and my dad in, *cariño*?"

Mac held on for a minute longer, then released Dirk and stepped back. "How? When? I thought you weren't coming?" Mac fired questions at him, then didn't even give him a chance to answer before she turned to face me. "You did this?"

I smiled. "I told you, *mi hermosa esposa*, I'd always give you what you needed."

"Evidently, it includes telling your brother it was time to quit feeling sorry for his damn self, pull his head out of his ass, and be thankful for the sister who loves him," Dirk said as he hobbled in on the crutches and my dad followed, shutting the door.

Mac stared at me, and I didn't know what to expect, but it sure wasn't the snort that came from her.

She continued to look at me as she spoke to Dirk, "Oh please, when did you hold back on what comes out of your mouth? I know my husband, and he wouldn't have put it *that* nicely."

I smirked and stuck out my hand. "Nice to meet you, man."

Dirk rested on his crutches while he reached out and clasped my hand.

"Same, man. Anyone who can put up with her has my respect."

"Don't be an asshole. Come on, and I'll introduce you to our boys and Kiyaya. Then you can sit and tell me how your trip was," Mac said and led the way into the living room.

Introductions were made, and after setting my dad and Dirk up with a cup of coffee, the present opening began. What had taken Mac hours to get wrapped was destroyed in no time. Wrapping paper, boxes, clothes, and toys littered the living room floor.

Later, after the mess had been cleaned up, and we consumed the tons of food Mac made for dinner, my brothers had stopped by one by one with their women to meet Mac's brother.

Mac and I sat in the living room and watched Tracker and Paxton play video games with Dirk. Kiyaya had gone upstairs to lie down, and my dad had gone to meet with the other dads to share a beer to celebrate the day.

"He's lost so much weight," Mac whispered beside me.

"He'll gain it back, along with his strength. He's still recovering, *cariño*. Give him time. By this time next year, I bet he's back to the way you remember him."

"Not all the way, though." I knew she referred to the missing part of his leg.

"He'll adjust, and so will you."

"Something else is on his mind, though. Maybe he's worried about what he's going to do after he's medically discharged." Mac sighed and laid her head on my shoulder.

"More than likely," I answered with no intention of sharing with Mac what I thought was going on. I'd noticed, too, but I didn't think it had anything to do with adjusting to having a prosthetic or being discharged from the military. My guess, it involved a woman.

"Have I told you today that I love you?" Mac said as she lifted her head and turned to look at me.

I kissed her, and when I broke the kiss, I leaned my forehead on hers and answered, "Yes, and I hope to hear you say it a lot over the next fifty years."

"I'm not sure that's long enough to love you," she said, then leaned in and planted a kiss on lips. When she pulled away, she added, "It will probably take me that long to get used to your arrogant ass."

I chuckled, then pushed her head back down on my shoulder. I might have said I wanted what my brothers had found, but as I held Mac close and watched Tracker lean over to help Paxton with the controller—I realized I had found much more.

Epilogue

Flirt

I walked into the waiting room on the delivery floor and looked around. My brothers were there with their women and kids. Ally sat between Crusher and Carly, her legs swinging back and forth as she shifted in the seat.

"How long do babies take?" Ally asked Carly, and I smiled.

"Well, some come quickly, and others take a while. It depends on how badly they want to come out and meet everyone," Carly answered her.

"Well, if they don't want to come out, why did they go in there in the first place, Dad?" Paxton looked up at Coast and asked from his seat between Coast and Tracker.

I sat down on the other side of my brother. "That's new," I commented.

Coast and Mac had filled out adoption papers a month after they started fostering Tracker and Paxton. They didn't tell the boys, though. My brother didn't want to jinx it. He'd said if they shared with the boys and were denied, he feared it would set back the progress they had made with them. After the holidays, they'd gotten the call, and not only had they cleared, they had been given a date for the four of them to go before the judge to make it official.

Two weeks ago, we all sat in the courtroom and watched our brother and Mac officially become Tracker and Paxton's parents. The ICWA social worker from the reservation smiled and congratulated them. She'd been a big supporter of the adoption.

It hadn't hurt that the boys had thrived living with Mac and Coast. Tracker's grades in school were excellent and above average. And Paxton was doing just as well in first grade. It helped he was at the elementary school where Ally went, and River taught.

"Yeah, it happened last week. No fanfare or anything. Saturday morning, Paxton got up and came downstairs. Mac and I were in the kitchen, and he looked at Mac and said, *What's for breakfast, Mommie?'* She spilled her coffee all over the table and while she was wiping it up, trying to hold herself together, Tracker walked in and said, *What did you spill, Mom?'* That did it, brother. She shoved the rag at me and mumbled she'd be right back and fled the kitchen. I got the cereal and milk out. Gave the boys each a bowl and spoon, then went to find her. She was in our bedroom crying her eyes out. By that evening, they were calling me dad, and

226

I'm not ashamed to tell you it brought a lump to my throat. Best feeling, brother."

"I'm happy for you and glad everything worked out."

"Thanks. Can you believe Sami and Luna went into labor on the same day? This shit is crazy," Coast said and shook his head.

"It is. Was Mac worried about Luna being early?" I asked. Ghost had lost his first wife and son in a car accident. He joined Black Hawk to work on healing from the loss. I knew my friend had to be worried.

"She told me on the way here that it isn't uncommon for twins to come early. Before you arrived, she told us that both Luna and Sami were doing well. She said the twins were okay, and she didn't foresee an issue."

"Damn, I'm glad."

"Dad," Paxton said, and Coast looked over at the boy.

"Yeah, Pax."

"I asked you, why do babies go in there if they don't want to come out?" Paxton asked again, since Coast hadn't answered the first time.

I chuckled. "Yeah, why do they do it, brother?"

Coast turned his head back to me and glared. "Seriously?"

"You aren't going to be able to put it off. Not with the way the women are dropping them," I said and smiled.

Coast had told us at the shop one day that Paxton asked Mac how she gets the babies out of their mommies. She explained birth so a seven-year-old would understand, but when he followed up and asked how they got in there in the first place, she distracted him with cake and told Coast that was his job. It'd been weeks ago, and evidently, he still hadn't sat Paxton down.

"I'll get to it. Don't worry about it," Coast grumbled and turned back to Paxton.

"Mommies and daddies get together, and their love puts a baby in the mommy's belly," Ally piped in.

I knew then it was going to turn bad. And no sooner than I thought about it. It happened.

"They don't have to love each other. He just needs to stick his dick in—" Tracker stopped before he finished when Coast shoved on his shoulder.

"You finish that, and I'm going to take the Xbox away," Coast said.

I put a fist to my mouth and feigned a cough to cover my laughter. Devil, Jag, and Crusher, on the other hand, didn't have a problem laughing out loud.

River, who sat beside Jag with Poppy on his lap, rubbed her belly, then slapped Jag's arm. "You won't think it is funny when Poppy says stuff like that or our son," she pointed to her stomach.

Bailey looked at River from her spot. She sat on one side of Neely while Devil sat on the other side of the little girl. "I'd reach over and smack Lance, but we all know the chance of this one…" She rubbed her stomach. "*not* saying or doing inappropriate things is a stretch, and we'd all be in denial." Every one of us laughed at Devil's expense.

"When the babies get here, the boys are going to outnumber the girls five to three. Seven to three once River and Bailey deliver," I said.

"Girls still rule anyway, Uncle Flirt," Neely said.

"No, they don't," Paxton argued.

"Bailey said so, and she's right, and you're not," Neely argued back.

"Guys are always right," Tracker said, backing Paxton up, showing loyalty to his brother. But I shook my head and leaned back in the chair because Tracker was going to get a lesson that nothing good came from saying stuff like that to women. Even small ones.

"Are not!" Ally stood, and so did Neely. Poppy, barely over a year, clapped her hands and watched from Jag's lap. Yeah, that had to be a bad sign.

"We're stronger and smarter, which makes us right," Tracker sneered, and Neely lunged. The only thing that kept her from getting to Tracker was Devil's fast response time, grabbing the back of her shirt.

I glanced at Coast. "Brother, you going to step in?"

"He's going to have to learn. Might as well be today. It will save him a shit ton of trouble with women when he's older."

"True."

"You didn't have to stop her. She's just a girl. I wouldn't hurt her," Tracker looked at Devil and said.

Christ, there was a good chance we were all going to be kicked out of the hospital.

Devil smiled. "I wasn't worried about you hurting her, Trac. I was worried about her hurting you."

Tracker looked at Neely, and she grinned at him.

"Aunt Carly says that boys aren't smarter than girls because they don't think with their brains. They think with their penises," Ally sneered at Tracker.

"Ally, your mom has told you a hundred times. You're not supposed to repeat what grownups say."

"Really, babe. You picked that one to go with?" Crushed said to Carly and lifted a brow at her.

I leaned closer to Coast and lowered my voice, "You know, it's probably a good thing the boys are going to outnumber the girls—they're going to need those numbers to survive against them."

"I agree. The teenage years on the compound should be interesting," Coast said.

"Yes, but chances are it will all work out. Our dads lived through it," I said.

"Yeah, but there weren't any girls in the mix."

I didn't have time to reply. Mac walked in, and the room went quiet.

She grinned widely. "Black Hawk MC has three new members. Archer Weston at eight pounds, twelve ounces and twenty-two inches long. Lock Carver at six pounds, two ounces and eighteen and a half inches long. And Key Carver at an even six pounds and eighteen inches long. Mothers and babies are all fine. And both dads stayed on their feet."

Everyone hooped and hollered, and I watched as Coast went and hugged Mac. When everyone settled down,

Mac added, "After the parents and babies have time alone, you'll be able to go back. Ally, honey, you get to come with me now to meet your brother."

Ally jumped from her seat and grabbed hold of the hand Mac held out. After they left, everyone started talking, and Crusher pulled out his phone and started texting. The dads had left that morning on a ride to Canada and when the women went into labor, they'd turned around. The hospital would be the first place they stopped as they rode into town.

I leaned my head against the wall behind me and watched my brothers interact with their families. We'd been together since the day each of us was born. They were my club brothers, the brothers of my heart, and my best friends. I'd witness each one fall as their woman entered their life.

Leaving me, the last man standing.

Acknowledgments

To all my readers – Thank you!

Carson

About the Author

Carson lives in the South with a Great Dane and two adopted shelter dogs that keep the household in line. Books have always been a part of her life. There is nothing better to her than curling up and relaxing with a good story and losing herself in someone else's world for a few hours.

She enjoys writing romance with a real feel to the stories. Writing with the belief not every man is a jerk and not every woman needs saving.

Writing and growing as an author with each book is her goal. She wants to reach the level where a reader knows when they see her name, they can trust there will be a good story as they flip through the pages.

Carson's been on her writing journey for a few years. As she's finally settling in, her only regret is she hadn't started sooner.

To stay up to date with Carson – visit her website- https://carsonmackenzieauthor.com/ or sign up for her newsletter- https://landing.mailerlite.com/webforms/landing/l2k1l8.

Books by Carson Mackenzie

Black Hawk MC

Speed
Crusher
Devil
Ghost
Jag
Coast
Flirt

Haven MC

Moose's Regret
Hawk's Bounty
Keg's Revelation

Desert Phoenix MC

Desert Phoenix Rising

Standalones

Her Way or No Way
two paths One destiny

Boxed Sets

Black Hawk MC Books 1-3
Black Hawk MC Books 4-7
Haven MC Books 1-3

www.ingramcontent.com/pod-product-compliance
Lightning Source LLC
Chambersburg PA
CBHW020406210626
46816CB00006BB/2146

9 781952 184369